THE

SAVED

A.L. YOUNG

THE SAVED

THE BLUE LATTICE NETWORK

BOOK TWO

A. L. YOUNG

ISBN(Hardback): 979-8-3302-0882-1

ISBN(Paperback): 979-8-9880030-7-6

Audio Narration By: Star Willams

Cover design by Get Covers

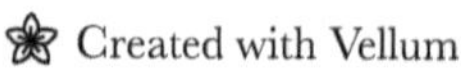 Created with Vellum

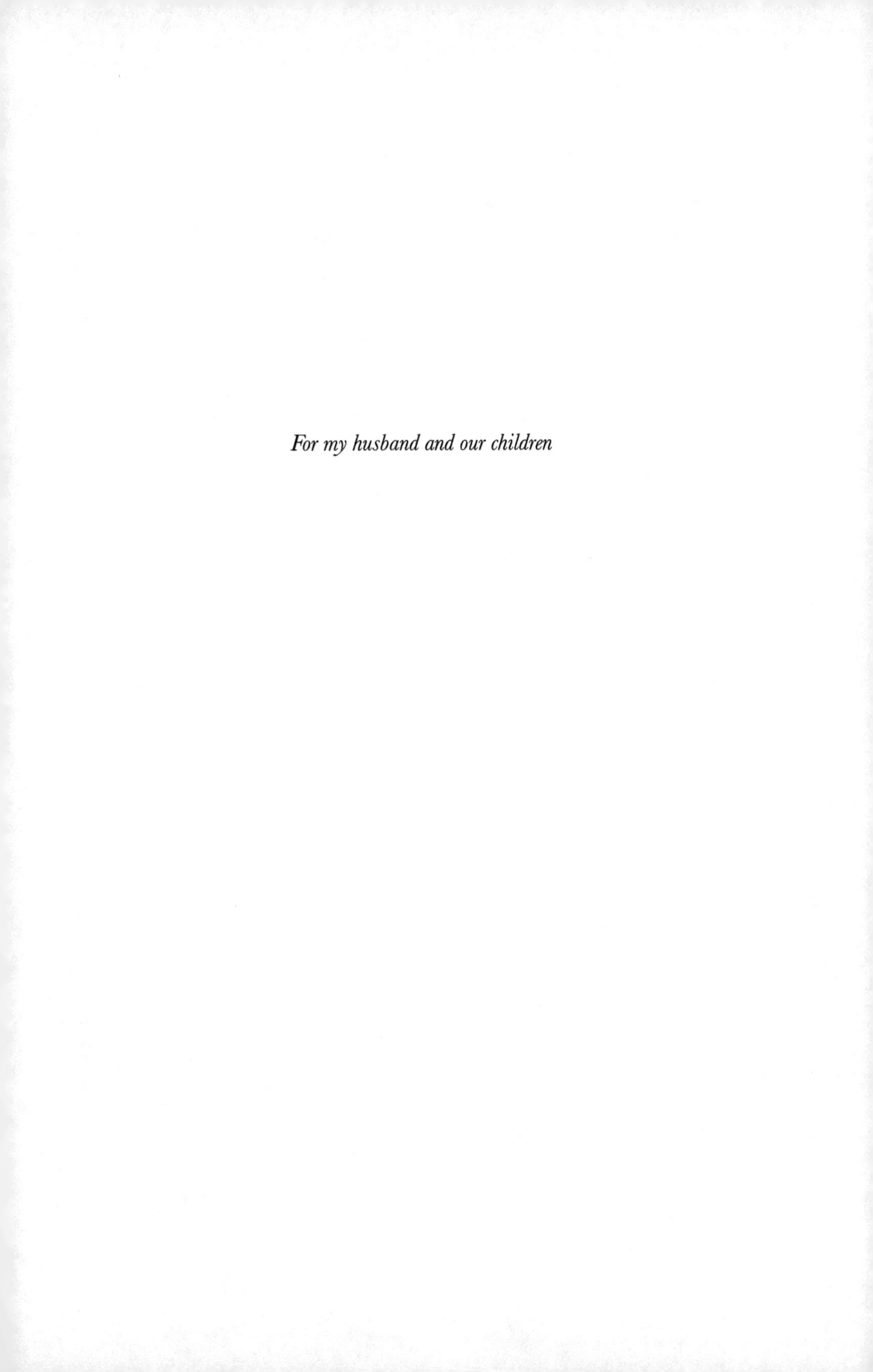

For my husband and our children

About the Book

This book contains graphic depictions and/or mentions of drug use, adoptee trauma, closed and open-door casual sex, police encounters , mass child death, hospitalization, trafficking, slave auction, enslavement, the death of a parent, parental manipulation and coercion, bribery, medical trauma, chronic pain, murder, knife violence, and gore and blood. If you are sensitive to such material, proceed with caution. Your mental health matters.

Cadril

Cadril
BYWUL
Red Pond
Nordale
Beech coast
New Pine
SALTEZ
Silverwild
Star Rose
ARESTOMER
Glass Hill
MAYKIS ISLE
Somber
Upper North Vale
LUCENT
Tol
TALIS
Misepeek
Tundra Woods
South Vale
Mouse
GRASSHOPPER
Cedar Wood
Amaryllis
Boye
RAVEN
May Hills
South Hills
Willow Port
Crow Feather
CROW
Diamond Sea
Turpeek
City Center
Moss Point
ROBIN
Bell Whispers
BLUEBIRD
Clayton
Anvil
Ivy Ladder
PHOENIX
Hush
EAGLE
Ocul
Bayville
Lance Bank
Kroft
N
S

CONTENTS

THE SAVED

THE SAVED

WAKE

Amethyst

In a hazy half-sleep Amethyst heard a knock at the door. It was soft and polite. She sat up and let the comforter fall all around her in a heap. She wasn't expecting anyone, but she also hadn't seen anyone in days. So, she figured it might be someone important. Maybe Zircon was making sure that she was still alive. Or Sasha asking her if he could eat her snacks. Less important but still important. She got up and opened the door and found nothing but a letter. It was an off-white letter with a black ribbon tied around it. She didn't pick it up immediately because she could hear, although softly a hush conversation. She walked down the stairs, following the voices. Sasha was there in the doorway talking to a man, Amethyst could only see his legs and shoes before the door was shut and Sasha turned around.

"Who was that?" Amethyst said.

"I…I don't know. He just said he had to speak with you and left you a letter."

"That's weird."

"Trust me I know. I couldn't even tell from his facial expressions what his business was."

"Is he still outside?"

Sasha opened the door and shook his head no, "the car is gone."

"He left so abruptly. I didn't even have a minute to open the door" Amethyst said as she fully descended the stairs. Amethyst spent the last couple of moments trying to remember when she heard the knock at the door. The last month she had spent in a complete haze. She lost sense of where one moment began and when another ended. She just remembers going to Judy's gravesite and the rest is a blur. She remembers being on the patio but the conversation or anything else that occurred is anyone's guess. What she knew, something that she could not shake out her mind was Sasha was Half-Blessed and it was her fault. This played in her mind at all hours of the night. The only time she got reprieve was when she was so tired that she could no longer keep her eyes open.

Sasha noticed her lack of focus and came closer. When things were completely still he would lose Amethyst to her own mind. It is happening more often these days. Sasha took her hand and led her to the kitchen. Zircon had already left for the day. She was at Diamond Sea with a guy she met a couple of weeks ago through mutual friends. He would feed her and then attempt to have the conversation again.

The air smelled of warm cinnamon and honey as he baked the pastries in the oven. Amethyst was still in her own world watching the birds' flit from one branch to the next. She folded her arms and laid her head down on the kitchen island playing with stray hairs.

Amethyst noticed the second bird perched on the thickest branch was a Crow at that moment. In its talons was a bundle of buttons and beads on a piece of white string. All of them were iridescent. The pastries were competing with the scene before her.

"Sasha look!"

"What?"

"The crow in the window!" Amethyst pointed to the bird and Sasha nodded.

"It comes around from time to time. I'm surprised you noticed it this time." Sasha turned off the oven.

The meal was eaten in silence. The bird was long gone.

Amethyst couldn't believe she hadn't noticed it before. It was so technicolor, so vibrant, why didn't she notice it? But that was a long time ago now. She was noticing now and she wished Sasha would give her some credit for at least that. She was trying to get better. She really was trying.

Amethyst picked up the letter off the floor and took it down to the living room figuring it would be easier to face whatever it was in the company of another person. The letter itself smelled of lavender oil. The ribbon laid unraveled in Amethyst's palm.

"I'm afraid of what it could be," Amethyst said to Sasha, as she sat on the couch.

"I'm here if it's anything unpleasant."

Amethyst slowly opened the flap of the envelope and was then disappointed when it was obvious, she wasn't able to discern anything from the tri-folded letter. She handed Sasha the envelope and opened the letter.

Dear Amethyst Millen,

Our firm would like to discuss the matter of your inheritance as the role as the head of your family line. Please call 404-683 to procure materials related to this position.

. . .

Mr. Field Maykis

The letter was confusing. What materials would she need to be the head of her family? Sasha asked her how she was now the head of the family if Zircon was the oldest and Amethyst explained that she was the youngest, so she was the only one able to have children.

"Able to by law or physically able to?"

"I'm not sure to be honest. I really don't want to know, to be perfectly honest."

"Do you think this Maykis has any relation to Ronald Maykis?" Sasha said, looking down at the letter on the table.

"I don't know," Amethyst shook her head.

The conversation unfortunately for Sasha ended there and Amethyst took her place back in her room and shut the door.

Holding On

Zora

Four IV's were running at the same time. Occasionally one would beep, and the nurse would replace it with another bag. Zora felt bloated but the fluids couldn't stop. The pain was simply at bay but not all encompassing like it was weeks ago but the way they talked about her was almost in the past tense. *She's holding on. She's holding on. She's holding on.* She heard that phrase in her half-awake state countless times. When she was able to stay awake, she was dizzy and even in her dreams she was dizzy. She couldn't read any of the labels on the bags as they were written in Crow. A language that was an odd mix of Roman alphabet and shapes. The nurses mostly spoke Crow between each other.

Today was a Wednesday and it had been three weeks since she was admitted to the hospital. She internally shook when she thought about how many times, she was stuck with another needle to replace an old IV. She tried her best to keep the current IV in her arm straight so it wouldn't blow, and they would have to replace it. The one in her arm was placed by the vascular access team and was good for a number of weeks. She heard her adoptive mom mentioned around the hospital a couple times, but she didn't know in what context it was being spoken.

The only thing was sure of was that there was Cerplex in her body and they were trying their best to rid her system of it. She thought about Muse a lot and she was angry that no one would tell her what happened to her or explain further about what happened beyond what she could piece together herself.

When lunch arrived, Zora tried her best to sit up. She didn't remember what she ordered. She just knew she ordered a side of tea and mashed potatoes. Everything else on the menu was foods she never heard of. She took a sip of tea. Her hands were slightly trembling.

"Would you like some help?"the nurse asked. Zora shook her head no and continued to sip. She sat the cup down and began on the mashed potatoes, and took a few spoonfuls to prove to the nurse that she didn't need any help. If Zora wanted anything, she wanted answers.

The skinny of what she knew was that she was transferred to a hospital in Diamond Sea after a trial had failed. She experienced cardiac arrest. Her heart made it out somewhere between fine and somewhat concerning. Sasha's dad Marcus Ashford was the one who was the head of that research, and it involved the use of Cerplex. No one had explained why she was being drugged and what exactly they were trying to cure. Zora took another bite and shook her head as if she could reset her mind of the stress.

She took the green plastic dome of the entree and realized she had ordered baked chicken the night before. She finished it, her hands still trembling, dropping the fork on her plate and tray a couple of times.

"Zor-ra" she spoke out loud to remind herself.

CARNATIONS

Muse

Days moved by slowly in this part of the world. They were agonizingly long. She wasn't told much besides that she would be taken to Crow Feather to be reunited with her birth mom but they were still trying their best to make the arrangements. Diamond Sea, where she was, was far from Crow Feather she surmised from conversations with the doctors who would come talk with her every day around 6 AM. Muse spent the better part of her day retwisting her natural curls with droplets of water from a paper cup. She was almost done with her head after three straight days of working on it. It was hard with all the fluids being pumped into her that made her feel a little loopy and her hands trembled when she would lift them.

Doing something with her hands made her less nervous though. Running her hands through her hair was as close to a warm hug as she could get. She wanted to know where Zora was, but they wouldn't talk to her about her when she would ask. Patient confidentiality perhaps but the least they could do was tell her if Zora was alive. Muse didn't remember much of that night besides falling on the ground and waking up restrained. Whatever drug they put in her system made her want to claw off her skin. When she asked what the drug, they put in her she didn't recognize the name. It must have been something only used in the Crow Territory.

Her cousin, Harlow, who was on her way to become a pharmacist some years ago would ask Muse to quiz her. She learned the name of so many drugs that way. The interesting sounding ones she would look up to find out what they actually did. The one her cousin kept forgetting was Cerplex. It wasn't talked about very much because it was such a controversial drug. Often given to prisoners and people on parole. Mind control drug was the easiest way to describe it but it did so much more than simply make someone compliant to demands. It hijacked the brain in so many ways. A person would rarely be aware of just how much the person who was prescribing it had over their choices. Another nickname was the "suggestion drug" but the impulsive way people would follow instructions given under the influence of Cerplex was far stronger than the word "suggestion" implied. It was used in nearly all of the territories but mostly in the Crow and Robin territory. She learned that from a random article dated back ten years ago, if it was still accurate was unknown to her.

Muse missed her nice clothes and her bedroom that was bathed in daylight. The entire right side of the updated Victorian mansion was a window segmented by rays of dark wood beams. She mostly sat in bed; the drug they were using to keep her well had the effect of leaving a person unsteady on their feet. She had been wearing the same white and gray striped hospital gown for the last two days. Periodically the nurse would come in and ask her if she needed anything. Often the answer was no but sometimes it would be help to the bathroom or ice water. The day was punctuated with those two needs when she wasn't eating.

Occasionally she would get so bored she would look out of the window into the courtyard down below. She wasn't allowed to leave the wing, but a lot of other patients were allowed to take strolls around the courtyard. The pathways were arranged like rays of light before they met in the middle and twisted up like a rope in a bow tie. In the very middle were pink carnations. Muse just sat on this occasion though, feeling the beeping of machines reverberating in her skull and the harsh glow of the fluorescent lights playing on her skin. She didn't know how she could explain any of it. Every doctor she explained this to dismissed it as just a common symptom of the drug. Some people, they said, felt extra sensitive to stimuli.

3 WEEKS, 2 DAYS

Zora

It had been a total of three weeks and two days. She sat up more now, still dizzy but able to stay up for longer periods of time. There was mention of her going home but Zora knew that meant she would go home with not the mom she had grown to know but a stranger. She didn't want to be seen like this in a hospital gown with half her panties showing, especially not by a stranger that wasn't a medical professional. The meeting wouldn't be on equal footing. To possibly be seen so vulnerable made Zora's stomach turn. She'd try to rehearse in her head what she would say to this woman about letting her go but the words never materialized. Outside of her door there was hardly any noise and she realized when she went to the bathroom that the girls that were directly across from her had gone. She tried to peek to see if the room next door to them was empty as well, but she heard shuffling of feet, and the question was therefore answered.

The previous night had been a tough one. She had broken out in a cold sweat and could already feel fatigue setting in as if she had a cold. She wasn't sure if it was the drug that constantly pumped through her system or the actual common cold. Or worse yet, the flu. She didn't divulge any of this to the doctor though.

Slowly she lowered the head of the bed, so she didn't have to physically do anything. This kept the dizziness at bay. It was too early for a nap and so close to having her vitals checked again but Zora couldn't help but to cat nap. Her eyelids felt heavy and her limbs like they were filled with hot sand.

She dreamed of nothing, but she did think of many things. Like where was Amethyst and Muse? She didn't want to even say his name out loud in her mind out of fear of conjuring his physical form, but it did appear as an ever so fleeting thought. *Sasha.* She realized she felt nothing but revulsion from the name. It wasn't an easy transformation. At first, she spent the better part of her time trying not to think about him. If she did find herself thinking of him, all her thoughts would swirl as if in a vortex and she would be unable to think of anything else. He would materialize and the things they would do together in private would invade her dreams. She couldn't believe she let him know her that way.

Zora didn't think much about the press conference back in February until months after when she began to be lifted out of his influence and from the effects of Cerplex. Under the influence of the drug every thought became an obsession. Out of the haze of the drug, everything seemed extra bright and every other sense extra sharp. Her thoughts completed themselves at a much faster pace and her emotions swung from each extreme like a pendulum.

Her first night at the hospital she nearly had a full-on panic attack. Her heartbeat so erratically out of her chest that she broke out in sweats and no amount of crying seemed to assuage the fear lodged in her throat. Things got duller and more normal after a couple of weeks, but as of now she was on one drug she knew to be for anxiety. When it was under control like it was now, she would think back to the protest at the Maykis Statue and the following press conference and try to make one plus one equal three. The only way any of it made sense was that Sasha knew more than he was letting on. Or at the very least he was very lucky. She thought the former more than the latter. When she was about to go back to her thoughts about Sasha the doctor showed up with the nurse. Dr. Brenner had skin almost as dark as hers and similar dark thick eyebrows. His smile was only slight, and his voice was warm and inviting.

"Looks like today is the day, how do you feel?"

"Fine," Zora lied.

"I'll have the nurse get your discharge papers together and take out that IV."

"Can I go home?" Zora raised her voice just a little, hopeful but not that hopeful.

"With your birth parents, yes."

"But I'm 20."

"Still a minor in this territory I'm afraid."

"When will I meet these mythical parents?"

"Parent. And very soon. She's in the Maykis Wing. He's at home."

Zora couldn't fully comprehend his words. She knew that she had other parents for a very long time. It was no secret that she wasn't a Jo'nest. She was given the family name of her adoptive father. But nonetheless her bluebird mother liked to pretend when people would ask, especially if they were rude or intrusive about it. Zora did share a complexion with her but that was about it. The nurse left and came back quickly with a transparent blue bag with the hospital logo with the words patients' belongings written in white bold letters. All the clothes she was wearing the night she fainted.

"I'll leave you to it," Dr. Brennen said as he made his way out of the room. The nurse left again for a moment and came back into the room with a small bag of supplies. Zora let her arm lay across the food tray so she could get to work at removing the IV.

NOT A CARE

Amethyst

She often tried her best to not pry into Sasha's mind when they weren't talking but, on this occasion, she was too tired to talk and just wanted to know what he thought. Some of the thoughts he had were what he was going to eat next and worrying but honestly just being frustrated with her.

She just lays there. I just want to pull her bed. She slept for eleven hours yesterday.

She actually didn't sleep for eleven hours yesterday. It was closer to six. The other hours she was daydreaming and that must have been what he saw. Amethyst hadn't even laid down yet, but she was ever so tempted. The fact that Zircon was giving her space was a big reason she was so tempted day to day just to melt into bed and never reemerge. Zircon said she didn't care what Amethyst did and Amethyst resolved not to care either.

DISCHARGE

Zora

A pair of dark denim jeans and a peach-colored top and a pair of sneakers with silver and pink details. Her red sweater was in the bag as well, but it would be in the 80s, and no need for it. She really wished she had something to cover the bandage and thick stack of gauze that was at the junction of her arm. Maybe she would wear the sweater. Zora did not want to sit on the bed. She didn't want to be seen in that position. So, she sat where guests sat and plopped herself on the recliner. She looked at her hands folded in her lap and focused on her breathing. It almost didn't feel real. It felt like she was trapped in a dream world. Every single shuffling of feet or opening or closing of doors made her feel on edge. When no one came right away she looked up at the ceiling, looking at the off-white terrazzo pattern. She took a few more deep breaths.

"*Zorah*," she heard someone say. She looked down to see a small dark complected woman wearing a floor length dress and her hair in a long braid swept to the side, any stray hairs kept in place by two bejeweled hairpins. Her eyes were a startling contrast and were baby blue.

Zora stood. She didn't walk to her right way even though she wanted to leave as quickly as possible. The sooner she could leave, the sooner she could try to escape and go back. The woman's long peach dress nearly touched the floor and as she walked a step or two closer to close the gap, she would pick it up and let it drop. Zora couldn't move. She found herself affixed in place.

"Hello," Zora said, trying to stop her in her tracks.

"You still have your accent," the woman said.

Zora didn't ask a follow up question. When the space between them was closed by a few more steps, Zora could smell the perfume she wore. It smelled woodsy and floral. Zora recognized the scent, but she said nothing.

"Are you ready?"

Zora shut her eyes for a minute and let out a ragged breath. Zora nodded yes and followed the woman out of her hospital room 106B, down the hall, down the elevator to the lobby from the sixth floor and to a small red car. Zora sat in the passenger seat. Nothing was said but she let the woman hold her hand the car ride.

WELCOME TO CROW FEATHER

Zora

Every so often they would pass by a green sign that read how many miles they were from major cities. Turpeek was nearly sixty miles away, which meant Bluebird Stream was over double of that. She would need a car. There were no train lines that connected this part of the territory to the Bluebird Territory. The thought made her mind feel heavy and nervousness was cropping up in her stomach.

"I've missed you." The woman said as she continued to drive.

She wanted to leave the car at that very moment. Her hand felt sweaty. She felt like she might throw up and everything just smelled and felt so different.

A big red sign that read "Welcome to Crow Feather" took all the space of what she could see. Zora's heart sank. They were at the very top of the territory. Closer to Willow Port in the Raven territory than anywhere near the Bluebird Territory.

. . .

The drive continued until the scenery changed from woods to waterfront and boardwalks. They drove up a narrow road off the highway and came upon a small cobblestone house that was covered on the right side with ivy. A small round window peeking through. The roof itself was thatched. The woman pulled up to the garage. She pushed a button on a small remote on her keys still in the ignition and the white door to the garage.

"I'll let you get settled. I'd imagine you're hungry. We've been driving for hours."

Zora didn't feel hungry. She felt on edge. She felt like her nerves were frayed wires. The woman parked the car in the garage and left the car to open Zora's. Zora's legs felt like jello from the long ride that she nearly fell face forward when she was climbing out. The pair went through the door of the garage and were in an empty storage room and through another door and up narrow stairs was the kitchen. Zora noticed the round window she had seen from the outside.

"Are you hungry?" The woman asked as she was walking over to the refrigerator.

Zora shook her head no and the woman sat at the dark blue kitchen island. Everything was a dark, rich blue. The appliances, the island, the walls. Zora found it all ironic.

"Zorah" the woman said.

"It's Zora" Zora spoke up, not adding that god awful "R" sound to the end. It rang in her head like a dull bell.

"Zora." The woman corrected herself, but it seemed to make her uncomfortable.

"I'm Eliza, but you can call me mom if you like. I can't fully realize how hard this is for you but I know it must be. You can call your mom if you like. I honestly don't mind it." Eliza spoke with a deep reverence but there was also a hurt behind her words that Zora couldn't ignore.

"I want to leave," Zora finally spoke up.

"You may leave but first we need to do something." Eliza said.

"What?" Zora asked, curious.

"I know you've been experiencing the pain for quite some time. I know the way to make it stop. It's important that we do this soon. There might not be another opportunity. The treatment that they gave you in the hospital saved us some time. It's almost like setting back the clock but soon we'll run out of that time."

"I don't understand."

"Being a Crow isn't just a nationality. I think you understand as much as that? Right? There's a special ceremony we perform when our children are close to the majority age. It gives you the ability to continue our bloodline and it allows me to move on." Eliza got up from the kitchen island and walked closer to Zora.

"What do you mean by move on?"

"It allows me to die."

"What? Are you joking? Are you trying to trick me?" Zora couldn't help herself.

"I'm not trying to trick you. I hear that it's relatively peaceful. After I'm…gone you'll be in the care of your uncle until you reach majority. I'm sure he'll be okay with you leaving to sort out your affairs once you complete the ceremony."

"What exactly do I have to do?"

"We have to go to a special pond. You simply have to submerge yourself in it and wait until you hear a voice. I don't know what it would sound like. You simply have to trust your gut."

"Where is this magic pond?"Zora regretted how she sounded but it was too late to take the attitude back.

"They're scattered around. There's one in Crow Feather."

How convenient.

"Why do you have to die? Why can't we just not do…" but Zora couldn't finish the thought because she intimately knew why they couldn't wait. The pain was excruciating.

"You weren't meant to experience this kind of pain. It's only because they didn't return you and your peers soon enough. It was never meant to be this way. It was supposed to be peaceful."

"What about the ones who died?"

"Well, their parents are now immortal."

. . .

Zora considered her words, why wouldn't someone want to be immortal? I mean watching one's child die was the obvious reason not to desire that, but what about the ones who never had children, what became of them?

"What if someone just didn't have children?"

"They wouldn't die if they were biologically Crow. Not all Crows are biologically Crow. Some are just residents."

"Is this a secret?" It sounded dumb to her as soon as the words left her mouth, but she had to be sure.

"Yes,the people who need to know currently know or will know."

"So basically, all the pain I was put through could've been avoided a long time ago. Like when I was fifteen?"

"Fifteen?" A confused look spread across Eliza's features.

"Yes, that's when I started feeling the pain." Zora said.

"It's not supposed to start that young."

"Well, when is it supposed to start?"

"Closer to eighteen." Eliza shook her head.

"What's wrong?"

"I don't know. I don't know how you are going about your life experiencing such pain for so long. I'm so sorry Zora."

"I'm here. I'm fine." But thinking about it Zora could feel the prickly sensation on her cheeks and around her eyes. She felt like she could cry but absolutely refused to. It also made her aware of the hunger she was beginning to feel.

"I think I'll take you up on some food," Zora said as she further closed the space between them. Eliza nodded and opened the fridge. Everything was neatly organized into glass storage containers with rubber gray closures. She began to take out a couple of containers of various sizes and sat them onto the kitchen counter next to the fridge.

She didn't smell very much until the food was hot. It was a mix of lavender, hot oil and spices. She didn't think as she ate. Zora only focused on what she was experiencing on her tongue at the moment.

The first taste was fish, underneath the skin was a salty paste. The next was a cornmeal mush that had bits of peppers and scallions. On the side were pickled onions. She didn't really touch them. Eliza simply watched Zora eat.

Eliza took Zora around the second floor where her room was and the shared bathroom. The bathroom was the size of a bedroom and the bedroom the size of a closet. Her bed was nestled in a small nook with a window.

"I'm sorry it's so small but we needed the space for your father."

"Where is he?"

"He'll be back soon."

"Okay," Zora sat on the bed, the springs cradling her.

"Is there anything you need?"

" No, I don't think so," Zora lied. What she needed was to be out of the room and in the warm air outside so she could fully expand her lungs. Eliza left her and Zora laid down on the bed. The scents, the light and surroundings, all unfamiliar.

SOCIAL WORKER

Muse

The day had come, and Muse was on edge the entire time. The nurse had already given her the discharge paperwork and her clothing. It had been washed, the ghost of a bloodstain on the t-shirt still there but a very light brown. An hour passed before a social worker appeared from behind the partition. She had curly dirty blonde hair and wore a light brown pantsuit with a white and cream pinstripe blouse. She talked for a while, but Muse didn't pay attention until the very end when she said they would be driving together to her mother's home. They left the hospital and went past two very large parking lots before coming upon her car. It was a large dark gray SUV. It was a little difficult to climb into the SUV with the pain that still sat underneath her skin.

"What do you listen to? News, easy listening?"

"I'm okay," Muse said as she buckled herself in.

They drove in complete silence. The only sounds were the sound of the car driving over the places where the metal plates met together on the highway and bridges and the rattling of metal gates. The social worker who Muse didn't know the name of was happy the entire ride. It unsettled her.

When the woods turned into beaches, Muse's stomach lurched. She didn't realize just how far on the edge of Crow Feather they were going. They drove down a narrow road that seemed to wind back and forth like a snake traveling across grass. They came upon a large gray Victorian mansion with a red roof.

Next to the detached garage was a fleet of obviously expensive cars she couldn't name. Everything looked new. They left the SUV and walked toward the front door. Before they could knock, a maid who very well might have been watching opened the door.

"I'll leave you here." The social worker said. She placed her hand on Muse's shoulder and gave a soft squeeze.

The maid had long dark hair and skin that had a honey-like glow.

"Please come in," she said as she opened the door further.

The living room was on the right side of a grand dark wood staircase. It wasn't simply one organized sitting area but a handful of small seating areas like one would see in a dorm room common area. Muse sat on the couch closest to the window and simply waited for this figurative woman to appear. She only waited for a few moments before she heard the click of heels coming down the stairs.

"Ms." The maid said, she held out her hand, Muse stood up and followed the maid back to the foot of the staircase. She had long curly hair like Muse but everything about her curls were perfect. Her skin was the same porcelain white as hers but not a blemish. Her eyes were a dark brown, much darker than Muse's hazel eyes.

"Muse?"

"Yes," Muse said.

They went to the deck on the opposite side of the house. The woman didn't say much to Muse. The maid worked quickly to put out a full spread of small cakes and cookies on three tier platters.

"If there's anything else you'd like, just let Merit know."

Muse nodded yes and rested her hands in her lap. The woman talked about the weather like it was any other day. She went on to talk about sports which Muse couldn't follow.

Muse just sat there and nodded. It was like watching a vision of her future self talk right in front of her.

"What is your name?" Muse's voice was barely a whisper.

"To you I'm mom but to everyone else, Ava."

Ava. Muse tried saying the name in her head to see if it rang any bells and it didn't. It sounded just as foreign as anything else. The mom that raised her didn't look like her much at all, but they did seem to share the same large eye shape. But this woman, her actual mom, looked like an older version of herself and she couldn't ignore that fact at all. Anyone seeing them side by side would be able to tell they were related. Her own name, *Ava* didn't seem suitable for such beauty. This woman didn't look like she was anywhere near as old as she should be, having a 21-year-old daughter. Knowing all of this, it just felt odd to say the word mom in the presence of her. It had been too long of calling the woman who raised her mom that it almost seemed like total disrespect to call anyone else this. Something else was nagging at her too. Ava seemed to have more money than she knew what to do with and even she couldn't seem to do much of anything to get Muse back before this. Muse didn't want to think about what that could've looked like when she was five- or ten-year-old or even fifteen. The thought made her so uncomfortable. The Bluebird Territory seem to have more power than she initially realized, and the thought made her shutter.

MACHINES

Zora

So many machines. Beeping and beeping. This was not how she expected to meet her father. He was in the largest room in the house she was told, hooked up to every machine imaginable. Lining the wall were faded rubber duck shapes. The former nursery, her nursery. He was waking up. Eliza pushed Zora up to him.

"His vision isn't the best. You're gonna have to go a little closer."

Zora wore a blue surgical mask. Eliza told her his immune system was a little fragile. What would be the point of all this, would he even recognize her? But she decided that thought wasn't fair. He wasn't dumb. He could put two and two together. His skin was as clear as her mother's but broken down where the IVs were taped down. When he opened his eyes, the shade was a deep brown, the same set she looked into every day. Not quite like chocolate no…like coffee. They were like freshly brewed arabica beans. He didn't say anything, but his heart rate jumped a bit, the machine glowing red with a warning.

"Zorah." He nodded as if he were agreeing with himself.

"Yes, it's her," Eliza said, pushing Zora even closer to the hospital bed.

"Hello." Zora wanted to say more but she stopped herself mid syllable.

"How have you been?" the man said so casually like they were sitting right across from each other about to enjoy a cup of coffee.

"Better," Zora answered honestly.

He nodded, considering her words, and said "we have a lot to catch up on. I've missed you *so* much" He took a deep breath in and let it out as a sigh.

"Yes, we do," Zora spoke softly. He looked so old despite having such a young complexion. No, not quite, he seemed so frail was the right assessment. Zora remembered Eliza's words as that thought was fleeing and another was beginning. He would die as well and the thought that followed was, was he waiting this whole time for this? Was her very existence keeping him alive? But that didn't seem so because he seemed so sick. Zora guessed it was mostly his sheer will and not simply her existence but honestly, she didn't know. She didn't understand how any of this worked.

"We have many things to celebrate. In a few days, you'll be 21." He continued.

Zora had completely forgotten that her birthday was coming up.

"Maybe we can order a cake from Mary Beth's," Eliza said as she went around the bed to the other side. She shifted his pillows, so his head was more propped up and adjusted the head of the bed, so he sat at nearly a 90-degree angle.

"Last time we went there, Zora. You were one."

"Zora?" He said, and then continued, "Zora," as if teaching himself her new name.

"Yes, Zora."

"I can live with that. As long as you're with me." He spoke.

"But I won't…" Zora started but immediately stopped herself.

"Yes, yes, I know it won't be forever, but any moment is enough for me. I can leave knowing you're safely sleeping in your bed in this house."

"But why?" Zora felt an uncomfortable feeling creep across her spine. She still didn't understand why any of this had to happen.

"Magic is finite. It needs to be taken back to dole out to new souls."

Zora didn't doubt his words. It was the casual way in which he spoke them that made her not question him.

"If it's so finite, why did so many children…" she trailed off.

"Why were there so many children affected by the famine? We used to have more children who would continue the family lines. There used to be more family lines: *Klide, Clover, Janis*…they're dying out. There are far fewer families than there were in the past to put it simply. It only seems like a lot because there are so few children in the Bluebird territory. You can thank TerraTech for making so many of those women infertile."

"What do you mean?"

"There was a drug, Cliopriem that was used for your typical menstrual cramps that turned out it disrupted the cycle completely with prolonged use. They tried to repackage it for birth control, but it was far stronger than that. They took it off the market when they noticed a steep decline in births."

This was the first time Zora was hearing of any of this.

"This was back in the 2030s. TerraTech bought the patents to the drug and slapped a new label on it. Gave it to female inmates instead. It's just illegal for doctors who don't deal with that population to prescribe it."

"See-lee…"Zora started.

"See-lo-li-pri-em," He corrected, his voice reverent.

"Why is this the first time I'm ever hearing about this?"

"It's the territory's greatest shame. They stigmatize women who can't reproduce as if that's the only thing a woman can do. And if they can't keep up with other territories in that department, who will replace their aging population? The famine in a lot of ways was a way for the Bluebirds to reclaim their standing. They didn't like that Crows and even Robins were outpacing them."

"Robins?"

"Yes," Eliza answered.

"How does any of this work?" Zora already knew but she wanted to hear him say the same thing.

"You'll basically dunk yourself in one of the special ponds that still have the magic. It only takes a moment and from there you have to wait to hear your guide say something. Sometimes it's a string of words, sometimes it's a hum or a song. It will be something for your ears only. And when you emerge, all the pain you've been experiencing will end there. You'll be healed from anything you might die from."

"If that's true then why are you sick?" Zora sounded harsh but things didn't seem to add up.

"My transformation wasn't done by my mom. It was done by my cousin. I've been looking for a way to fix it for quite some time. But now that you're here my mother and father can go on as well."

"So, someone else could, do it?"

"No, no. No one else should do it. That's the perfect way to end your family line. Especially if you're a woman. Men, the only effect it has is it makes you prone to all the illnesses and diseases that humans are able to have. If you try to get anyone to do it, you put them in danger of illness if they're a man and stuck alive if they're a woman. It stops all things. Understand?"

Zora immediately knew what he meant by 'stops all things' ; it would make her unable to have children of her own. It would freeze her in time. The thought made her dizzy.

"The implications of the action are grave, Zora."

The warning he gave was not lost on her.

FEAR

Muse

The pond was shaped like a kidney bean. They stared at it from atop a hill. Every so often their feet would crunch on some sand that was tracked up from the beach. There was no cover from the sun's unrelenting rays. It was just the three of them, Muse, her mom and Merit. During the drive up, her mom told her to keep an open mind but as they came upon the body of water, all she could think about was drowning. Muse hated the water. She hated baths. She barely tolerated showers. Anything that put her in close proximity to the element she greatly disliked. Each time she was near it one of her earliest memories would resurface. The beach. 2060. And the feeling of a ball lodged in her throat each time she had the urge to swallow another mouthful of water to try to combat the feeling of suffocation. As they came closer Muse could feel her heartbeat hard in her chest, nearly rattling inside its own cage. She took a deep breath but everything inside her screamed to walk the other way. She couldn't stop herself even though she wanted to run away.

When they made it to the edge of the water Muse recognized the scent. It was rose water, the same scent her mom would dab behind her ears before parties. There were so many parties. This rose water scent though, smelled much more light and pleasant to the senses then the one her mother would often wear.

Before she could utter a word, her mom was right behind her, putting her hair into a high bun. Muse said nothing. She would allow it. She couldn't remember the last time someone was this close to her that wasn't a nurse or a doctor. Something inside of her craved this interaction. The way her hands gently caressed her scalp felt nice. When she was done she touched both of Muse's shoulders and sighed.

"Ready?"

"I guess."

Her mom took off her clearly expensive shoes and began walking toward the middle of the pond. Her body half submerged in the slightly murky body of water. Muse peered into the water, seeing tiny fish swirling around the bottom. She was grateful she could somewhat see the bottom. Perhaps it was somewhat clean.

"Come to the middle, Muse."

It was clearly a command. The look on her face was serious but Muse couldn't make her feet go forward.

"It's only a few feet deep." Her tone was much softer.

Muse walked in a bit, and then walked back. Taking her shoes off at the edge she continued. When the water reached her shins she stopped again. This felt like it would take all day. The element felt alien to her. She hadn't been this deep in a long time. It felt soft which was an odd feeling, almost conflicting with the other sensory switches of wetness and cold.

"Are you afraid of water, Muse?"

Muse nodded. The temperature of her face turned up a few degrees.

"Come, come. Hold my hand."

As if that would help.

Muse nonetheless nodded and took another baby step, her hand a clear three paces from her mom's but still outstretched. Another step and their fingers brushed against each other's.

Another step, and her mom bent over a bit and gave a soft tug, enough that it slightly pulled Muse forward. Now an arm's length away, Muse was motivated to take another step. She was there now, in the very center.

"I need you to do me a favor. It will only take a moment. I want you to go under the water, just for a moment and *listen* very carefully."

Muse was ready to turn back around, but the combination of the water weight of her clothes and the fact she didn't have car keys to go and then drive away was keeping her firmly in place. She felt trapped.

"It will only take a moment."

Muse shook her head no.

"Why do I have to do this?"

The question seemed to catch her off guard. She looked nervous.

"I know you've been experiencing pain for some time now, right? They had tried to stop it at the research center and it didn't work, right? This will end all that. No Cerplex. No other drugs. No hospital stays."

"How?"

"This pond is sacred. It runs on a finite magic source. It has healing properties."

"Magic is finite?"

It sounded so foreign to her ears. The magic that she thought of was conjured up and at the ready to anyone, just a wand and maybe some herbs and special words. It wasn't a pond. The only magical water she could think of was holy water. But that wasn't exactly magic. Not in the theatrical sense i.e. movies.

"Magic…needs to be transferred. I'm transferring mine to you."

"Oh, okay." There was nothing else she could think to say. The fact that she walked out into the middle of a pond with murky water wearing a nice skirt suit was enough for Muse to believe what she was saying. Even if it wasn't true, and didn't work, the most that would happen was she would get very wet but that alone seemed like such a tall order. Even with the promise of magic. Whatever it meant.

"If you don't do it, you will die. Like the fallen children."

It had been so long since anyone had mentioned them. It was like it was a distant memory even though it occurred only a few short years ago. She was in the library when it happened. She was trying to check out a book when the girl running the circulation desk began to grasp at her notebook. She took a pen and when she couldn't right it upward in her hand she put her hands around her throat to indicate she was choking.

Before Muse could do anything the girl was on the floor, dead. The entire library was covered with scattered bodies. All of them her age. The connection wasn't made until many months later when TerraTech started doing their research on the deaths. All the children who fell, or teens rather were adoptees. They all were from the Crow territory. The gene responsible was discovered and named 8alpha6 and sequenced and tests to detect it were developed. After two years the test was perfected to such a degree that it could be done at home or at school or on the roadside. Wherever it was needed. Muse just always assumed it was some kind of defect because of the famine and what had caused the famine.

"There's nothing wrong with you." Her mom said, seeming to read her mind.

"Just go underwater for a moment and that's it?"

"And *listen*."

Her body fought her part of the way but Muse obeyed. She let the water pool around, first her elbows and then her shoulders and finally her head. When she was fully submerged, she felt a warmth. Perhaps it was the sun. Perhaps not. But there was definitely something different about the water. Something purer about it than any other body of water she had ever been in. The smell of rose water seemed to coat every molecule of water. But softly she heard a melody. The beginning of a song that was deep and sad. It ended as quickly as it began. She listened again, wanting to be certain that was it. No other sound but the sloshing of water beside her as her mom touched her shoulder, signaling that she could come up. Muse didn't want to resurface. She wanted to hear the song again. But her mom tugged again, more forcefully and Muse, running out of air, came up. Her breath came out in pants. Her mom embraced her. Speaking softly, she said thank you.

To be Here

Zora

In two days would be the day they would go to the pond and Zora's whole stomach was in knots with anticipation. Now though they would spend time together. Tomorrow was her birthday and Eliza was going about the house getting things ready for her uncle that lived a few miles up the road. It was long overdue that they should reunite. It wouldn't be quite a party. It was more of a get together of sorts. In the back of Zora's mind, she still thought about what should happen if she left. After the dunking of course but immediately after. She didn't want to think about what should happen after and wondered if it happened within twenty-four hours or if it took days. She didn't want to know. She could sleep soundly in ignorance of it.

~

Eliza was cutting flowers over the sink and a thought crept into Zora's mind that funerals often have beautiful flowers like those. When she was done Eliza put them into a crystal vase. The vase had a 3d image of a tiger cradling a flower she couldn't name, its body outstretched like it was reaching for a football at the other end of the field but instead of a ball it was the flower. It was a beautiful image.

"Your father brought me this a long time ago when we visited Kinder Pond," Eliza said as she turned on the cold water. She let it run for a few moments before testing it with her hand. She let it run into the vase and then shut it off. She headed over to the fridge and took out a tray of ice. She turned it in on itself and plopped a few ice cubes into the vase. She placed the vase in the center of the kitchen table on the other side of the kitchen. It was dark blue like the rest of the kitchen but instead of being blank it had tons of little yellow, red and white flowers over its surface. The design was very Scandinavian.

Back in the room Zora felt useless. She couldn't do anything about the ceremony, and she couldn't do anything to stop Eliza from throwing the small get together. When she would try to broach the subject Eliza would bring up another thing she had to do. If it wasn't cleaning, it was cooking and if it wasn't the two aforementioned things, it was people to call. It was beginning to sound like there would be more people.

The room wasn't anything special. It looked to be a guest room. The sheets were nice though, soft and smelled of lavender. The walls were a canary yellow and the blankets at the foot of the bed matched. The bed was made of a dark wood with carved rose bulbs at its' post. The window was draped in a thin linen curtain with an eyelet trim. The edges of the room where the baseboards met the floors were a little dusty and it made Zora sneeze.

June 5, 2070

Muse

The silence in the room didn't match the inside of Muse's head which was screaming at her to finally say something. To explain herself. To possibly get herself out of trouble. But she didn't. The adults continued to talk mostly among each other about what she had done. The word expulsion was batted around by the Dean Yolanda U. and head of students, Maxine Janis. Janis kept repeating that this kind of behavior would've gotten her banned from campuses territory-wide if she were in the Crow Territory. Muse knew what she did was wrong, but she couldn't help but to laugh at the facial expression of the student in her mind's eye. Their dorm room was covered in cups of cooking oil spread in every open square inch. Janis called the act "destruction of school property" though none of the cups had spilled. Muse sat on her own bed as the other student(Millie) who shared the room with her pick up and dumped each cup in a bucket. This was at three in the morning. It lasted until nearly five in the morning. Muse still hadn't explained why she did this and she really didn't want to.

"Are you listening to anything they're saying, Muse?" Her mom said.

"Yes," Muse lied. She learned to tune out adults. All they tended to do was yell at her anyway.

"Well, what do you have to say about this? You made that poor girl clean all of that mess up. What if she fell? What if she hurt herself? Then, what? Were you gonna take her to the hospital?" Her mom continued.

"She was fine." Muse countered.

"MUSE!" Janis practically yelled.

"Okay. Okay. I'm sorry I made her clean it up." Muse said softly now. She really didn't expect her to clean the entire dorm room. But that won't matter to them because according to any adult anything Muse seemed to cook up in her brain was bad to begin with and always would be. She didn't want to keep talking about it. She wanted out of this room.

"I'm sorry," Muse muttered under her breath. But this utterance was too late. The adults were already talking about her expulsion in more specifics. Littlewood Academy was brought up. She had never heard of it.

"She would have to commute from the suburbs to the town but there's a pretty small student community, she shouldn't be able to get away with too much," Ms. U said as she got up from her desk. Janis was walking toward the hall opposite the desk to the student files. She didn't have to go very far to find the last name Drew.

"I'll fax this over with the transfer form. We should know within a few weeks if they have the space in their next term."

"I think that this is all too much for what I did. No one got hurt."

"Your behavior has been regularly questionable in the last few months. Your grades alone are enough to get you expelled. I'm sorry, this is it."

In the parking garage they walked down the stairs to level C where Muse's mom had parked. The garage shared its' body with the stables. The two conjoined structures sharing a concrete wall. They would drive up to Howard Hall and clear out her dorm room. There wasn't much on her mind but if she would take all of her books or not. It wouldn't all fit in the SUV.

Her room was on the fifth floor and her roommate was already gone today for her final. It was just Muse and her mom. The room was for the most part bare on the left side which was here with the exception of the books all over her bed and stuffed into the small 3-shelf bookshelf all students were allotted. Muse started with her bed, stripping it bare. And then she stuffed all her toiletries from her desk into her plastic caddy. Her mom was emptying the drawers and putting it into her suitcase. Her mom worked quickly, as if she worked slowly the embarrassment would catch up to them.

"Can we slow down?" Muse said as she her trembling hands were organizing her pens into the large case on her bed. *Why were there so many pens?*

"I'd love to finish this before that poor girl comes back."

"I don't care what she thinks."

"I do."

Muse blinked back the tears that were forming in the corners of her eyes as she zipped up the pouch.

"We only have two hours." Muse said as she made her way to the corkboard above her bed. She took down the pictures, some of them being popped off before the pushpin was fully dislodged.

"I can't believe you, Muse. I feel like it's every three weeks I'm up here trying to talk down the dean to not get you expelled and now you've finally done it. Why? That's what I wanna know. Why?"

Muse's whole frame was vibrating with anger now. Not at her mom but at herself. She didn't know. She couldn't control herself. She didn't understand why she couldn't stop herself that night. Something had taken over her brain in those moments as she went to the store, bought the oil and filled dozens of cups one by one.

"I don't know." Muse said, softly. The beginning of crying strained her speech.

Her mom put her light brown hair behind her ears and continued to pack, ignoring Muse completely.

～

The entire left side of the room was bare with the exception of the white sheets and gray blanket which belonged to the school. Muse shut the door. She only had a small rolling suitcase left, her mom had already gone down in a couple of trips with the rest of her things. The excess of books were left in a box at the end of the hall.

They drove home. The drive took close to an hour. Muse didn't say goodbye to anyone and a part of her regretted it but another part of her was thinking about the two finals she had to finish in order to be a senior at her new school. The sign marking the yellow riding trail was the last she saw of Hollow Grove School.

Zora and Muse

Zora

The nurse was remaking the bed when she came in. Her dad sat in a wheelchair at the foot of it.

"Zora. Good morning." He said. His large dark brown eyes had a glint of excitement.

Zora nodded, she was full of breakfast and trying to keep everything down. Her mom was still in the kitchen doing clean up from breakfast. She could hear the constant running of water. It was just her and her dad.

"How are you?"

"Fine. Fine. Today is a better day. Twenty-one. How does it feel?"

"Good."

It really did feel good to have another birthday. For a moment there Zora thought her birthdays would stop while she was in the hospital. She would never openly admit that though. She didn't want to scare them. She closed the door behind her and walked next to him and watched the nurse make perfect corners with the thin white sheets.

"I tried to reign in your mom but I'm afraid tonight will be a little crowded." He sounded genuinely sorry about the big party Zora really didn't want.

"Don't worry about it." Zora decided she was going to worry about it all by herself. She didn't really know any of these people and now she was going to meet a bunch of strangers all by herself.

"There will be plenty of food to eat, your mom found a restaurant that does mostly Bluebird dishes. I know Crow food is quite pungent."

"I'm okay with Crow food," Zora said. It was starting to grow on her a bit and she didn't want them to go out of their way for her.

"No need for that. This is your day!" Her dad was clearly excited.

"Ava Janis is coming, she's the mayor of Crow Feather. She's bringing her daughter. Her daughter is also a former Bluebird."

Zora nodded, more to herself than her dad. The nurse was done then and she was coming toward them. She wheeled her dad to the bed and put her arms squarely underneath his. In one swift heave she had him on the edge of the bed. With a few more adjustments he was back laying down.

"When you taste the cake your mom brought, try to be impressed. She likes Mary Beth's but I think it's a little overrated."

"Okay, no problem." Zora laughed. It felt nice to laugh, even if it was a little bit.

"How did you sleep last night?"

"Terrible."

"Ah. I see."

"It's nothing," Zora said as she walked next to the bed.

She wasn't stressed about anything in particular but she simply couldn't settle her mind. She kept having thoughts about being in the hospital. None of the thoughts were particularly bad, they simply were dissecting what happened. She couldn't remember everything and that thought bothered her. She guessed she could get her medical records but did she really want to read what was in them.

"I was just thinking about the last few weeks…"Zora trailed off.

"Yeah, you had a rough go at it."

"Yeah."

. . .

Zora sat with him until he drifted off to sleep.

~

In the kitchen Eliza was opening trays of food that had been delivered. The kitchen smelled heavily of warm chicken and buttered pastries and a stew which was a mix of herbal scents and carrots. The Crow food was on the stove still cooking. No one was expected to arrive for another hour or so. Zora sat at the kitchen table, holding a box that Eliza had given her. Zora knew what it was but she wasn't ready to undo the ribbon tie. She could read the stamp that read Pristine's. See the small rectangular shape and know it would be a mask. Eliza was wearing her own black mask and she was able to put two and two together.

"Do I have to wear it?"

"Hmm?" Eliza looked up from the stove to the kitchen table and shook her head no.

"Do I have to wear this?" Zora wanted further confirmation.

"No, you don't have to but a lot of people are going to."

Zora steeled herself as she untied the black ribbon that was keeping the top and bottom half together. The ribbon fell away on the table and she saw the mask nestle there, pitch black with two bright blue stripes at either end. Zora took it out with shaking hands. The smooth fabric falling through her fingers like water.

"Thank you." Zora said.

"No problem, Zora." Eliza said.

~

On the patio was where all the appetizers were. People had begun to arrive. First it was her uncle Eric. He was tall and slender like her dad but had more wrinkles around his large eyes. His build was also similar to Zora's. Athletic and thin. He sat next to Eliza on the lounge chair. In front of them was a faux fireplace that was a screen that lay flat that looked like they were watching a fire from above. It was nestled inside a cylinder of white smooth rocks. Zora sat in front of them, balancing a small plate of mini croissants on her leg.

"She's so mature now." Eric said as he took another sip of wine.

"Thank you," was all that Zora could think to say.

"You still have your accent." Eric said.

He was the second person to say this but she herself couldn't hear an accent in her own voice. She didn't say anything else at first. She was playing back the words she said in her own mind.

"Are you in school?"

"Talis University."

"Good school. We have a satellite campus near here for Maykis University. Perhaps you can continue."

She would have to redo the entire spring semester to graduate and the thought of doing it all over again made her stomach queasy. She would have to redo her capstone as well. She wasn't even sure if they would allow her to transfer considering she failed the entire spring semester at Talis because she was arrested.

"I don't think they'll let me transfer."

"Your record is clean. There's special exceptions made for adults who come back." Eliza said.

"Oh," this news was welcomed to her. She didn't know what she would do if she was basically regarded as a criminal for the rest of her natural life.

"Yeah, it would be unfair if we essentially punished all those children who didn't know the full story for the rest of their lives. That's madness."

"Do they have a journalism degree?" Zora sat up more.

"Yes." Eliza said.

"We can go and sort all of that soon." Eric said as he took another sip of red wine.

"How have you been?" Eric said to Eliza.

"I feel like I'm coming down with a cold but other than that I'm okay. What more can I want?" Eliza said.

It didn't immediately register in Zora's mind that Eliza was talking about her. She was still tired from hardly getting any sleep last night.

. . .

"Oh, I think I hear Ava's voice." Eliza said as she got up from the lounge sofa.

The door to the patio opened and Zora heard a familiar voice drift to her ears. At first she didn't move, feeling herself frozen in place but then she felt a hand on her shoulder.

"Zora." Muse said. It was a question that Zora answered by shaking her head yes before turning around and seeing her face.

Muse looked different. The embroidery floss was gone. Instead her own natural curls framed her round face. Zora got up so she could fully turn her body. Muse was wearing an outfit she had never seen before. A white eyelet dress. She matched the woman next to her. It must have been Ava.

"Aren't you beautiful…I'm Ava, you must be Zorah." Ava said.

A look of confusion washed over Muse's face.

"Just Zora," Zora corrected.

"Ah.I apologize, Zora." Ava said as she went over to the table and grabbed a glass of wine with her delicate right hand.

"You're okay." Zora said more to herself than to Muse. Muse nodded and closed the space between them.

"I'm okay." Muse looked as though she was about to cry but she didn't. She only embraced Zora.

"How long have you known my daughter?" Ava said as she took a seat.

"A year or so" Zora said, now realizing it was soon going to be two.

Muse didn't say anything, she simply stayed half in Zora's embrace looking up at her.

"Have you gotten in touch with Amethyst at all?" Muse said as she let her arms fall down at her sides.

"No, no." Zora said, grabbing Muse's hand and leading her over to the other side of the patio.

The adults continued their conversation and Zora and Muse were next to one of the outdoor torches.

"Sasha?" Muse whispered.

"I don't know." Zora answered back, her tone terse.

"Are you okay?" Muse's tone was gentle.

"I just don't want to talk about him, okay?" Zora sounded like she was asking permission to drop the topic.

"Last time I heard of him, he was still in the territory." Muse continued, "I'm surprised he didn't get arrested for Ivy Ladder."

"Really? Really Muse?" Zora whispered back.

"Yeah." Muse

"He's the son of a top TerraTech researcher. He clearly was protected from anything that we would be easily arrested for."

"I know but he was in it for us since the beginning. Why would he?" Muse stopped herself short.

Zora was about to say something, but she paused. It would be very mean of her to call Muse naive even if it were very true. There was something very pure about seeing the best in people and Zora didn't want to take that purity from Muse's heart even if Sasha was the last person on Earth to deserve it. Zora also couldn't be sure to be perfectly honest if Sasha was guilty of anything or just highly protected but in her head it really didn't matter. He should be suffering.

"Did you hear what I said?" Muse came closer.

"No, I didn't, I'm sorry. What did you say?"

"Isn't Sasha your boyfriend?"

"No. We're not like that." Zora felt a nervousness all over her body.

"Oh."

The party had migrated into the dining room. Eliza was getting the cake ready on the counter.

"Wine?" Ava said as she placed a glass in front of Zora.

Zora nodded yes. She didn't really care for wine, but she needed something to take some of this nervousness away. The wine was a sweet white wine. Zora liked it.

Eliza turned off the lights and began to sing happy birthday as she walked over to Zora.

The candles were round, thin, and white. The cake was chocolate with white chrysanthemums around the edge. Zora took in a deep breath and blew softly. With candles extinguished, the fragrance most associated with birthday cake filled the room. Eric smiled, putting his hands to his mouth and clapped. It looked as though he would cry but it was hard to tell in the dim light. Eliza and Zora's dad were on the same side of the table as Eric now and the look of delight on their faces was undeniable. Zora could only manage a small smile. A slight curvature of the lips was a more astute description. Muse looked lost in thought which was something that immediately worried Zora. Muse worried about things. That wasn't what worried her. It was the fact that it was happening meant Muse was pondering on something big. Muse was the kind of girl who didn't worry about what typical people worried about. Zora at first wasn't sure if it was because she was very smart or very dumb. Zora learned as she had gotten to know Muse that what she worried about was things people often didn't see coming until it was too late. It was Muse who predicted that TerraTech would start surveillance on students, and it was Muse who predicted TerraTech buying up property in the city square meant something unsavory was going to happen. Muse was right on both fronts.

Zora sat back in her chair feeling the nervousness come back and creep up her spine. She was running out of time and Muse would soon go back home with her other mom leaving Zora unable to pick her brain. Unless she found a way for Muse to stay and talk with her. Eliza left in that instant and came back a moment later with a cake knife and some small plates.

The cake was a deep rich chocolate with a slightly bitter node. It was delicious but not out of this world, but Zora remembered to compliment the cake when she ate it. Muse was sitting between Eliza and Ava, and she hadn't said much. It was clear to Zora then that Ava and Eliza were close friends. They laughed like schoolgirls in the yard. Zora took the opportunity then to grab Muse from between them. Muse said nothing as Zora took her hand and walked her into the hall adjoining the kitchen.

~

"What's up?" Muse said really casually.

"What do you think was up with Sasha?" Zora didn't want to waste any time.

"That's what I'm trying to figure out. Look, at Ivy Ladder when we were going to break the pane of glass—

"Shhh!" Zora couldn't believe how loud she was being about a literal crime. Their literal crimes.

"Sasha kissed me. He told me not to do what I was about to do, and he kissed me twice."

The first thought Zora had in her mind was she couldn't picture that. It wasn't that she didn't believe that Muse wasn't telling the truth. It was more of, she didn't believe that Sasha would try to manipulate Muse of all people that way. She didn't feel much else behind what Muse had said. She didn't have the same feelings for Sasha that she had in the past. Especially with everything that happened to her and didn't happen to him.

"It doesn't surprise me, Muse. He's a manipulator."

What Zora said seemed to hurt Muse's feelings because she took an unsteady step backward, nearly walking into the wall. *Did Muse have feelings for Sasha?*

"Muse, you don't think that Sasha has feelings for you?"

"No, Zora it's not that at all…I…I…just didn't think he would do that—

"To you?" Zora finished.

"Yeah."

"He does it to everyone."

THE CALL

Muse

She thought a bit about Zora's words, and it immediately made her wonder if that was what Sasha had been doing to Zora the whole time. Was he messing with her heart and mind the whole time? Did he have any feelings for her at all? Did he care about either of them, even if it was just as friends. Muse walked further backward and let her back rest against the wall.

"You okay?"

Muse nodded yes and took a few deep breaths to steady herself.

"Do you have his number?" Muse realized this was a stupid question after she asked it but she was unable to take it back.

"Yes. Why?" Zora said.

"Do you think he knows where Amethyst is?" Muse's eyes were wide as she spoke.

"Why would he know? Amethyst ran."

"Amethyst trusts Sasha though. She would've talked to him just like we talk to him."

"Her mom wouldn't let her though—"

"She didn't have to know."

"It's been months. She's probably in Arestromer."

"There are a lot of checkpoints between Moss Point and Arestromer. It's not unlikely that she didn't make it." Muse was irritated.

"No, no, you're right." Zora looked apologetic.

Even with just the two of them Zora's room was really crowded. Zora and Muse were waiting for her cell phone to charge. It was still in the bag labeled Patient's Belongings. She didn't have it on her at the research complex so the detective must have given it to the hospital. Something along those lines made sense. They didn't have the right adapter so separated it apart to plug it into the usb port on the outlet. It seems like it was taking forever to go from dead as a brick to enough percentage to make a call.

Muse sat on the bed looking around the room and Zora was directly next to the cell phone, leaning against the wall.

"How are you?" Muse realized she didn't really ask.

"I've been better."

"Fair," Muse replied.

"You?"

"I feel a little lighter. At least I know someone in this territory."

"Yeah, I guess you're right." Zora said, looking at the phone on the floor.

When the screen lit up the amount of text messages and alerts Zora had on her phone created a nearly endless song of chimes.

"Anything from Sasha?"

"No, no. My mom texted a lot. I should probably tell her I'm alive."

"Amethyst?"

"A couple times." Zora sounded surprised.

"What does it say?"

"*U there, are you okay?* and *We didn't make it to Arestromer. I'm in the Crow Territory. Text when you can.* The first text was from long after the protests at Ivy Ladder and the other was from last week."

"Text her!" Muse got up from the bed.

"I am I am," Zora's fingers were flying across the screen. The faux typewriter sound filled the small space.

"You should probably tell her we're both—"

"I am, muse."

CATCH UP

Amethyst

The sound of the text notification made Amethyst jump out of her sleep. It was nearly 10 at night and she had been in bed since 6.

Hi, it's Zora. I'm okay. Muse and I are in Crow Feather. It's a very long story. I'm sorry you couldn't make it.

The text seemed to revive something in her brain. She was awake now. She texted back.

I'm okay.

It was a lie but close enough to the truth at the same time. She was okay. She wasn't dead at the very least. Another text bubble appeared then.

. . .

Good, where in the Crow Territory?

Technically it was out of the city limits but Diamond Sea was the closest city.

Diamond Sea

There wasn't a reply right away and then a stream of text like a staircase.

Are you with your mom?
    Do you know where Sasha is at all?

The first question was like a punch in the gut. All those old memories surfaced; the emotions somewhat detached. She could still smell the rose water on her skin. She knew from watching his mind eye that Sasha was asleep. Having an odd dream that she couldn't piece together.

Sasha is asleep.
    I'm not with my mom. I'm with Sasha.

The text didn't come immediately after but ten minutes later.

Where is your mom?

Amethyst knew she wouldn't be able to fully explain what happened to Zora. She might not know yet and it truly wasn't Amethyst's place.

. . .

She passed away a few weeks ago.

Immediately a string of text. The phone was nearly buzzing with pings.

Was it through a ceremony at a pond?

Amethyst felt a weight lift off her shoulders.

Yes.

The Fuck Up

Zora

Muse was staring over her shoulder when she made the text and tears were falling from her face onto the sweater Zora's mom let her borrow. It dawned on her then that Muse didn't know. Muse read the text again to herself. Her voice was low and broke at the end.

"What does that mean? Does that mean what I think it means?"

Zora couldn't make herself talk. She found herself unable to dislodge the words from her throat. She shook her head yes and resolved not to say anything for a moment. Muse was going to learn at some point, Zora only wished it wasn't like this. *Why hadn't her mom explained anything to her?*

Muse didn't say anything more and just left the room, sliding from behind Zora on the bed. She didn't close the door on the way out and Zora could see her walk down the hall and down the stairs, wiping her face as she went. Zora ran after her then. They couldn't see her like that. Muse had to keep it under control. It would make a really awkward situation for everyone if Muse just launched at Ava.

"Wait, Muse."

. . .

But Muse didn't look back, she cried harder then, nearly falling down the stairs on her way down.

"Please, wait!" Zora was able to grab a hold of her forearm, but Muse wouldn't relent, and she was still trying to walk.

"Please don't say anything. You weren't supposed to find out this way. It was supposed to be between you and your mom, and I fucked it up, I'm so sorry."

"She told me *nothing*."

"Wait, what do you mean? She didn't tell you what would happen before the pond?"

"She didn't. She just said it would heal me. She didn't say she would die transferring her power to me."

"Oh, I'm so sorry." Zora said and she pulled Muse closer in an embrace.

"What is the fucking point?" Muse said, looking up at the ceiling.

"That we live." Zora admitted to herself mentally that what she had said was really cheesy although it was true.

"All I've had is a couple of days. How long does it take?" Muse said.

"I have no idea. I haven't done it yet."

"So, you're still in danger?"

"Only until tomorrow."

Muse nodded, a little calmer now. Muse covered her face and Zora took her to the bathroom on the floor to clean her face.

It was perfect timing when Muse returned to the kitchen because Ava was in her sweater about to get her. Muse still looked like she would cry but her face was dry. When Eric asked her if she was alright, she chalked it up to allergies.

They're in the Territory

Amethyst

She could no longer lay in bed. She went downstairs to wake Sasha. Her whole body felt as though it was vibrating with excitement. They weren't anywhere near them but Sasha would want to know that they were safe. Sasha was softly snoring. In the middle of a dream. His blond hair created a web on his left cheek. Amethyst waited until the dream took a lull and he was entering a lighter phase of sleep to wake him.

"Sasha?"

He opened his eyes slowly, they were slightly red.

"It's late, what's up?" Sasha looked around.

"Muse and Zora are in the territory. They're okay."

Sasha looked like he didn't immediately register her words. He just looked at her. Amethyst repeated himself and Sasha then nodded his head yes and he sat up on his arm.

"Zora?" Sasha finally said.

"And Muse." Amethyst didn't understand why he missed her name.

"I don't understand. They were arrested."

"Arrested for what?"

"You didn't hear? They tried to blow the center pane of glass at the Hunter's Point Mall in Ivy Ladder. They were stopped but I couldn't help them getting arrested."

"How could you prevent them getting arrested Sasha? It wasn't your fault."

Sasha looked like he was going to say something else but stopped himself.

"They're in Crow Feather."

"That's all the way up there." Sasha shook his head, "I'm gonna go back to bed. We'll talk about this in the morning."

Amethyst still wanted to talk but she realized it was late. She went back to the room and just sat on the bed, still basking in the good news. She didn't think much of what Sasha told her about Muse and Zora immediately after, but it was her next thought. That pane of glass had to weigh a lot. It would've released so much glass. It would've been the most dangerous thing they had ever done. The fire at the Maykis statue was pretty bad but that was a little bit more contained since the base of the storefronts and statue had the ability to extinguish a fire. Amethyst was glad their plan didn't come to fruition. They probably wouldn't have been set free. In the same breath she thought their actions reminded her of terrorist. She shook her head. She didn't want to think that about her friends.

Amethyst laid down and closed her eyes. In her head she saw Zora and Muse as she remembered them sitting in a cafe and talking about class. She let these thoughts lull her to sleep.

The Pond

Zora

The drive was short and quiet. They stopped on a sandy road below a steep hill. The sun was buried behind clouds. It wasn't supposed to rain but everything looked outside as though it might. Eliza turned off the car and looked at Zora who was on the passenger side. Zora was able to manage a small smile. Her dad didn't join them. He was in a deep sleep when they left. The ceremony was something, not quite private but a special event between child and mother. Even though he didn't need to be there, there was a part of her that wanted him there. Though she didn't say anything, Zora felt an immense amount of relief from finally being almost cured from the mysterious illness that caused her acute pain for more than two years.

The trek up the hill was slow. They paused every few paces to catch their breath. Once at the top of the hill they could see the kidney bean shaped pond. The wind rippled the surface like a sheet.

"You can go on ahead. Go to the center of the pond and I'll meet you there," Eliza said panting.

~

The scent of the water was hard to ignore. It was a strong floral fragrance, but Zora couldn't place the exact scent. The water was cold in some places and warmer in others. She could feel seaweed around her bare ankles. Eliza was soon walking into the pond. The tip of her long dark hair instantly became wet. There was a serene look that came across her face then. It made Zora uncomfortable because she didn't exactly feel the same way. She was excited. She was relieved. But she wasn't relaxed. It was the same kind of anxiety she would get when her other mom would take her to church. When they were trying out that lifestyle, it always made Zora feel like she was putting on a performance. She couldn't muster the same religiosity as them. No matter how much she read and how much she tried to pray. This was different though. This felt more immediate. There were no far-flung promises, only the immediate. The immediate transfer and the impending end to life.

When they both were in the middle, Zora spoke to herself to relax. Eliza told her to go completely under and listen. Zora slowly kneeled down until it was only her head above the water, she nodded and then continued, the murky liquid surrounding her entire being. Zora didn't hear anything at first. Only the bubbles her submerging body left in the water's wake. But then a song, a deeply sad song. She wanted to rise from the water immediately but there was a smaller part of her that could stay under all day just to hear it more. As soon as it started it stopped and Eliza was pulling on Zora to rise up from the water. She obeyed, feeling an emptiness in her chest. She tried to replicate the song in her head, but she couldn't. She quickly forgot the melody. All that was left was the feeling.

Zora felt bad for getting the seats wet but she guessed this was the status quo. They probably had detailing specials for after one transferred their magic to their children at car washing places. Eliza took a deep breath in and out immediately after. It was clear to Zora that she felt lighter and generally more at peace. Zora felt lighter too but another emotion that she couldn't name was creeping up in her gut.

At the house was a large group of people that Eliza invited but didn't tell Zora about until they were driving up. Zora hoped to see Muse, but Eliza said they couldn't make it when Eliza noticed Zora looking around in the crowd of people in the living room. On the coffee table were various cards of congratulations and condolences. Zora tried not to focus on them, but her attention continually was pulled back to thinking about the strangeness of it all. To mourn while someone was still living. To have a funeral while someone was still living. It all made Zora feel ill. The question on the forefront of her mind was how long the process took but no matter how much she tried to stop the gears in her mind from turning, they continued to turn and piece together that it must not have taken that long especially since the celebration of their life was put together so quickly.Crows seemed to have it down to a science.

There was a girl at the party that looked so much like Eliza that it must have been her niece. Same dark skin but with big dark brown eyes instead of blue. Zora couldn't help but to look on at the girl and how comfortable she looked about everything. Perhaps she didn't know. Perhaps she did and this was all normal for her. Either way, Zora was jealous of her circumstance. She wore a petal pink dress and her hair in two long braids on either side of her head. On the ends of her braids were cream-colored ribbons tied into knots and allowed to hang loose. She wore a mask as well, but hers' was all black and didn't have the blue stripe that Zora's had.

Eliza said as she passed Zora that there was food in the kitchen, and she should try the pastries. They were apparently from a new place up the road. Zora didn't have an appetite but she still went to the kitchen so she wouldn't have to watch the girl any longer. There was a large spread of cheeses and meats and pastries and cakes. The nurse had brought dad to the kitchen and he was having some cured meats and cheeses on a small white paper plate.

"Eat, enjoy yourself. It's your day too," he said as he took a bite of cheese. His walker was beside his chair. Zora wondered about how he got around the house.

Zora hadn't considered that it was her day. She would live. Why would she consider it her day when nothing of real consequence would happen to her? Zora shook her head mostly to herself.

"I think I need to lay down."

Back in the room it wasn't as quiet as she would've liked it to be. She could still hear the murmuring of conversations and music. It wasn't particularly loud, but she was able to make out the lyrics. She wished it was music without lyrics. Especially since she couldn't understand half the lyrics being that they were in Crow.

She had already washed and changed before most of the guests arrived and the temptation of just going to bed was very tempting.

Hunter's Point Mall

Amethyst

The dream began with the four of them in a cafe. Amethyst was eating something. She could almost taste the pastry in her dream. It flashed to them in a supermarket and Amethyst had the thought that she needed something called Princess Lettuce. It made no sense, but the dream continued. Amethyst had never been to Ivy Ladder before, but her brain made up as it went and filled in the blanks. She was in a mall. She was trying on shoes. But then a loud cracking sound seemed to shake her whole body. Silvery glass poured down from the ceiling like a waterfall. Then the screams. They sounded far away at first but were progressively getting louder.

With a start Amethyst woke up, seeing the sheet pulled up to her cheek and Sasha standing over her. He had seen everything. He was planning on waking her. Amethyst couldn't help the tears that were beginning to flow.

A Force to be Reckoned With

Muse

When she closed her eyes, she could still see the text staring back at her. Ava had not said anything for a while, but it seemed to be more out of fear than apology. Muse couldn't help but to scream, not at Ava, but at the circumstances. She only just got here and there already wasn't enough time. It felt as though she would never be able to gain her footing. She didn't want to pull her adoptive mom into this, she really couldn't explain anything to her anyway, but a part of Muse wanted to have someone else to talk to. Someone less central to the entire situation that would understand what it immediately felt like to be blindsided.

"Muse?" Ava spoke up, carefully moving closer to where Muse stood.

It sounded like a question and Muse didn't know how to answer. Was she supposed to say sorry? Was she supposed to apologize for how she reacted to the purposeful withholding of information? She yelled and guessed it was fair to apologize for that but for everything else, no, not at all.

"What?" Muse asked, wiping the tears from her face.

"I just want you to know that if I could go back, I would've told you the whole truth. I just didn't know if I told you the whole truth that you would go through with it. I was afraid that you would not do it and put yourself in danger. I'm sorry. I really am, Muse."

"Why?" Muse couldn't stop the tears that kept coming.

"I'm basically asking for your help to let me die. It's not unheard of that some children just run away and try to get their friends to do it so their parents live."

"If that's an option then why wouldn't—"Muse shook her head.

"It has devastating consequences. It's not a solution. The only solution to continue one's line is to transfer the magic." Ava walked closer to Muse until they were nearly toe to toe.

"How long has this been happening?"

"For a long time. Hundreds of years. It's a curse."

"Why hasn't anyone tried to break the curse?"

"You think it's that easy?" Ava scoffed, "I'm sorry," Ava continued.

"How long does it take?"

"A few days for our family line. It looks like the flu."

Muse was thankful it didn't happen in a particularly dramatic fashion, but she had never seen anyone die before. There was nothing she could do to prepare herself for what was happening to her mother's body as she spoke. She was beginning to look a little sick, a sheen was developing on her forehead.

Merit came in a couple moments later with a pitcher of water and cups. Ava had her stay with them, and they drank the water, not a word shared between them for what seemed like a while.

"Would you like me to get dinner ready now or later, Ms." Merit said as she took another sip of water.

"No, no. You rest for a little while. Later, I want you to show Muse around the mansion."

"Yes, I will." Merit responded quickly.

Muse didn't notice before, but she noticed now, a bracelet on Merit's wrist that had two super small green LED lights on it. She would have to ask about it later. She had never seen anything like it.

Merit led her to the kitchen and opened nearly every drawer and cupboard. It was useful because she previously had no idea where everything was, she greatly depended on Merit to make her meals. Next, they went upstairs to a study. Merit showed her a computer that had a digital searchable database of every book that was in the library that was conjoined by a red archway. Next, they went to a room that was on the third floor of the house. There was a large bed and a conjoined section that had a sitting area and a library with bookcases built into the walls. All the spines were in Crow. She could read none of it. Merit opened each door as they passed by them in the hall. Most of them were empty.

"The master of the house is away but he'll be home tonight."

"My father you mean?"

"Yes."

"What does he do?" Muse was curious what his occupation was that kept him away for long periods of time.

"He works for Maykis Industries. I'm unsure of his exact occupation but he does conferences often. It's usually the busiest around the summer and fall."

"Does he know I'm here?"

"Yes, he's known for a while you were in the territory."

"What's a while?"

"A few weeks."

"Oh," Muse didn't know why that information bothered her, but it undeniably did.

"What is that bracelet on your wrist?"

"It's a Laura bracelet."

Merit didn't look happy when she said that, but she continued walking down the hall, opening the doors as she went along. Muse followed.

"What does it do?"

"Listen, when you have a boyfriend, you can broach the subject then. I don't feel comfortable talking to you about it now."

Merit began walking the opposite direction to close the doors she opened for Muse's inspection purposes.

Muse decided to not ask any more questions about it. Something in her wanted to apologize but she didn't.

MERIT

The text came in at around eight at night. A little later than typical for him when he wanted Merit's attention. Merit showered before he was due to arrive and went up to the third floor to wait for him. From the window she could see the car weave around the other cars to park in a more accessible area. Merit began to get undressed, leaving only her black sports bra and matching underwear. Merit tried not to think about how this would most likely be the last time they would ever be together.

Lying in bed she couldn't help thinking about how she had talked to Muse, thinking perhaps she should have told her something. But no, Muse had already a lot that she needed to process, and Merit shouldn't add the fact that she was her father's mistress to it. She would discover it on her own if she were smart enough.

When he arrived Merit could hear his footfalls on the grand staircase softly at first but then became progressively louder. The bracelet vibrated from being turned on. Merit couldn't help but to feel excited. It was an odd feeling mixed with sadness. David was a man who wouldn't allow her to feel sad for the transfer of power but for now while she had the room to herself, she would allow herself permission to feel sad. A few tears escaped her eyes and settled onto the sheets. When David arrived, he was still holding his car keys in his hand. He put them on the dresser at the other end of the room. As he walked closer still Merit recognized the nervousness she often felt in his presence. It wasn't from danger. It was from worry that she wouldn't live up to whatever expectations he had for the night.

"Merit," His voice was low.

Merit looked up, his hazel eyes looking down at her. They were Muse's eyes. Merit closed her own eyes and shook her head, her resolve to calm her nerves faltering. His hand traveled from her arm to her thigh. They were still cold from the outside air and left goosebumps in their wake. There was hardly a chance for Merit to take a deep breath before he slid his hand between her legs.

"How have you been my dear?"

Merit nodded, knowing full well that he didn't want too long of a response. She was already somewhat slick in anticipation of him. It made it that much easier for him to slip a finger in but nonetheless she still grabbed his hand, nervous. David looked immediately worried and withdrew his finger, sitting beside her on the bed he peppered her hand with kisses.

"What is this about?" His tone was undeniably tender.

Merit considered lying but if she said it was nothing, there would hardly be any denying it though as her body would betray her in the end.

"Have you reunited with Muse?" Merit sat up.

"I will. I will." David said as he gently pushed Merit back on the bed.

Merit didn't like the answer, but it really wasn't her place to say anything about his personal affairs. Especially when it didn't concern her directly. She winced when he reinserted his fingers, not from pain but she didn't expect it to be that fast.

"Open wider," David said as he was beginning to rearrange her legs.

Merit did so and felt the new sensation blossom between her legs and lower stomach.

～

Merit waited in the kitchen for everyone to finish eating. It would be more dishes than typical, but she would rather do them now than wait for the morning. Ava was kind and ordered out so Merit could focus on her other duties. The conversation in the dining room sounded relatively calm so Merit decided to not worry about it. She hadn't had a second shower yet so she could still smell on her skin his scent. It was a deep smell of musk.

A moment later Ava came in with a bouquet of white roses. She placed them on the kitchen island and nodded to Merit to put them in a vase. Merit took out a pair of scissors from the drawer next to the stove to start cutting the thorns and tips off. When she was done cutting, she placed the vase next to the window where the breakfast nook was located. The roses smelled lovely. She realized then that she had never gotten flowers from anyone. This wouldn't be unheard of. David wasn't hers. But she still thought about that fact. She hadn't been with the family for long, but it was long enough that she developed feelings of worry and caring about what would happen to them. When she arrived at Ava's doorstep she had just arrived from the courthouse. Her punishment for her crimes being servitude rather than jail. At first, she had felt like she had gotten off easy until it was specified to her the servitude part could be interpreted a thousand different ways. She later learned some of these ways were also base. There really weren't laws in place that prevented the arrangement that David and Merit had. She had to initially consent to it of course but that didn't mean she didn't initially feel any pressure to do it. It kept her mostly in the house and she liked that aspect of it. Her time would be up in a year and that should be enough time for Muse to get her bearings.

Merit washed dishes as soft music played on the radio. She was supposed to be alone, but she found herself with company. Muse.

She sat at the breakfast nook, twirling her curly hair around her wrist and hand. Merit didn't want to look at her because all she saw was David. Muse looked relaxed though in spite of everything and that calmed her own nerves. As she was putting the dishes away David came in with a cake. He nodded toward the box to Merit and she, knowing all of the cues, took out small plates and a cake knife.

Ava came a few minutes later and all three of them ate cake. The cake itself was a simple flourless chocolate cake and smelled absolutely delicious. Merit couldn't ignore how it made her mouth water.

Her hands were a little raw from being in the water for such a long time. Back in her room she could slouch. She could loudly yawn. She could let hair hang in front of her face and it not have to be pulled back by a headband.

When she was about to undress there was a knock on the door. Merit answered it and was surprised to see David, his face slightly flushed. He'd probably been drinking.

"Come with me."

He led her back to the bedroom on the 3rd floor. He didn't instruct her to undress, instead he did this himself, unzipping her dress and peeling it from her body. It fell into a puddle at her ankles. Next was her slip. In the same fashion it was removed, slowly and carefully. David pushed her close to the edge of the bed and touched her in such a way that she understood she should bend over. Bent over the bed and still with everything he left on her body from earlier in the night Merit felt dirty. In a swift and fluid motion David took off her panties. He tossed them and they gently fell to the floor. Now exposed, Merit opened her legs wider for him. Without warning he slid his fingers between her need, touching the bundle of nerves that lived there. Merit jumped. He withdrew his fingers and replaced them with his mouth, sucking her mound In completely. Her heart felt like it was fighting its way up her throat. Moistened now, David took two fingers and stuck them back inside her deep. Merit could instantly feel the pleasure rippling through her body, from the tips of her fingers to her toes. Merit grabbed the bedspread, her hands twisted up in them like talons.

"Master," Merit moaned. He fingered her gently at first but once a sheen developed on his fingers he picked up the pace. Merit leaned into this thrust, her face flushed red. David didn't seem to like this because he held her body in place with his other hand on the small of her back so she wouldn't move. The frustration she felt was so strong. She wished he just turned the bracelet on.

"You'll come when I tell you to come."

"Yes," Merit was on the verge of tears, her breathing hitched.

"Yes to whom?"

"You, master."

LAURA BRACELET

Zircon

At first there was nothing but the clicking of the clock above the bed and the sound of a leaking faucet in the bathroom, the drops gathering in a circle around the rim only to fall hard into the porcelain bowl below. There was no mistaking the soft buzzing sound of the bracelet as he presented it to her, the two small green LED lights right next to each other in the middle and the square puzzle-like juncture a nail's length beyond that. Zircon presented her right wrist to him, and he obliged and slid the bracelet on, it shrinking to fit snugly on her.

Zircon hadn't thought about what this moment would be like, but she was thankful her nerves were calm. The nervousness stemming from her fear that he wouldn't find her all that interesting and leave her like the other boyfriends before him. But this time was different and there was a Laura bracelet on her wrist and flowers on the bedside table, two firsts at once. Timothy Talis was the younger brother of Luke Talis, the Crow Territory President. They hadn't yet made their relationship public, but it was bound to happen soon. Gossip magazines were already leaking pictures and making guesses on how serious the relationship was to them. Timothy outranked her by a lot. He wasn't one of the founding family lines of The Night Crows like she was, but he was among TerraTech elite, what one would deem new money. Their joining of forces would greatly solidify both of their ranks. This was her mother's last dream before she died, and Zircon was sad she wasn't able to witness any of it.

"Do you want to try the first setting?" Timothy said as he took out a small remote about the size of his thumb. Zircon nodded yes and Timothy obliged and pressed the remote once. The bracelet buzzed. It wasn't immediate, the feeling steadily built up between her legs. She breathed in deep, laying down to let the feeling envelop her. Timothy rearranged her legs so that he was directly between them, and he was staring down at her, his hazel eyes laser focused on her breathing. A Laura bracelet was a powerful tool. Too much of it was enough to knock someone unconscious from lack of oxygen. Zircon was trusting Timothy completely with this new ability to control the very pleasure center of her brain.

In the beginning all Zircon felt was a warmth between her legs and nothing more but then she felt an insistent pressure that she wasn't getting a release from, the feeling just out of reach.

"I want us to stop," Zircon said between panting breaths. Timothy turned off the bracelet and pulled her up, his hands under her arms so she had her balance.

"Are you okay?"

Zircon shook her head yes and took a deep breath.

"I'm okay," she said as she sat up straighter.

Timothy wasn't convinced of that. He gently grabbed her face in his hands and inspected her eyes, looking for what—he didn't immediately know. Timothy had spent a great deal of time among all sorts of people, young and old and he developed a knack for knowing when something was off with a person's disposition. Some would call this a gift. Zircon recoiled at his touch and retreated further back.

"Do you not trust me?" He really didn't want to know the answer, but he couldn't help but ask.

"I trust you; I just never gave myself to anyone so completely before." Zircon looked down and buried her head in her hands. As tempting as it was to want to take her hands away from her face Timothy resisted. He didn't want to potentially scare Zircon. Timothy knew who he was, and it came with a heaping dose of fear of which he wasn't able to prevent from complicating his relationships. Anyone intimately associated with him had to agree to a lot. Some of it obvious and much of it unspoken. It wasn't uncommon for high-ranking families to use Laura bracelets. It also wasn't uncommon that there would be a slow and very private courtship before anything was formally announced. The slow part did not apply to their courtship, but they did know each other for a long time before anything of note happened. It wasn't unheard of that everything that was private would come to the surface eventually, especially when it came to dating a TerraTech official.

Timothy wished he could just kiss her and calm her nerves, but he wasn't going to insult her intelligence like that. He knew it was complicated. It wouldn't be fair to lull her into a false sense of security.

Timothy sat before her and let her come down from what could only be aptly described as panic.

"Maybe we shouldn't do it this week." Zircon said as she emerged from her hands.

"If you'd like to wait. We can wait. But the papers will soon catch wind and we won't be able to control the narrative if they break the news before we do."

"Gossip magazines have already said as much," Zircon continued.

"They're not reputable like the *Quill Inquirer* or *Crow National*."

"I know. I know." Zircon seemed to repeat to herself like a mantra to calm her own nerves.

The fact that everyone she knew would know and everyone who knew would have an opinion shattered all her sense of self. She wasn't sure where he would end and she would begin. They would be a package deal and something about this filled her heart with horror.

Zircon, doing it more for her own nervousness than his own pleasure kissed Timothy on the lips then, quelling the word that was forming on his lips on contact.

"Where is this coming from?"

Zircon leaned in for another kiss, smiling against his lips before landing another.

THE REGISTRY

Amethyst

The dream wasn't inconsequential but she was trying her best to regard it as such. What else could she possibly do now? The near crime had almost occurred and she tried her best to be placated with that information. When she closed her eyes she was grateful she didn't see the waterfall of glass like she did in her dreams. When Sasha had come in the room Amethyst had felt so much relief that her dream wasn't real. But now sitting across from Sasha at the breakfast table Amethyst couldn't help but to think about how he was involved too. Sasha didn't look up at her. He seemed to be cooking up a response and Amethyst gave him his privacy.

"I had no idea about what Zora and Muse were planning. And if I did I would've stopped them" Sasha spoke up.

Amethyst wasn't sure if she entirely believed that. If she were honest with herself, she didn't know how deep this whole protest ring went.

"I just participated in them, Amethyst. I didn't plan a whole lot. I'm not. I wasn't that deep in it" he answered her thought.

"There isn't like a ring. There's just a bunch of little groups and we often overlap. But I wouldn't put people in danger like that" Sasha continued.

He seemed genuine. So Amethyst dropped it and went on to other subjects.

"I've been thinking a lot about the thing…I mean the predicament you're in and I think we need to involve Zircon. I know I told her I could handle this on my own but I think I was wrong to be so…rash" Amethyst sat up more, looking into Sasha eyes for any hint of agreement.

Sasha nodded and then rocked his folded hands back and forth, perhaps trying to refocus.

"It's what..I mean, I think that's smart but I'm not even sure Zircon even knows. And Eve only knows of the state of being Half-Blessed. We have no idea how to fix it or even who my parents are. We should start with the latter" Sasha nodded to himself in agreement.

"That would be nice to just start there but we don't even know your real name. The registry has no one named *Cayden Sasha Ashford* on it," Amethyst looked irritated.

"We could, we could ask my dad" Sasha said as he wiped the sweat that was on his brow.

"I'm sorry but your dad is a lunatic. Why would he even help us? What would we even be able to ask him? This is all top secret information."

"It is but I've already been in the Crow Territory for weeks and I'm stuck here. The law basically claims me in terms of belonging to my parents and the state now. The least he could do is give me my adoption papers."

"A normal person would give you your papers. A head TerraTech official that's obsessed with curing our kind would probably just kidnap you" Amethyst said to the air, just barely looking in Sasha's direction.

"You can't possibly believe that…"

"He wanted you to hold me down so he could take my blood and test it."

Sasha had almost forgotten about that.

"Your father wouldn't know boundaries if it bit him on the ass" Amethyst somewhat regretted being so vulgar about it but it had to be said.

"Maybe Hakeem would help us…" Sasha admitted to himself in his mind that even that was a crapshoot but nonetheless he said it anyway.

"Maybe."

But in her head she was thinking of the ways even that could go south. Amethyst wasn't kidding when she mentioned kidnapping. She truly believed that Marcus was capable of it.

"Okay. We'll keep looking at the registry. Maybe there's something we missed."

"Okay. I'm cool with that and if all else fails we'll ask for more help."

"From non dangerous people," Amethyst added. Sasha was irritated with her now.

"Sorry," Amethyst said, looking on at Sasha intently.

Sasha and Amethyst hadn't been in the study in weeks and immediately after opening the door they got a whiff of a rotting apple they had forgotten about. Once the table was clean they began organizing the files they accumulated by title.

The longest document was spiral bound. It was the name of every "Lost Child" as kept by the Crow government. Sasha was not on that roll but he was on the roll for children adopted after the famine as kept by the Bluebird government. They accessed that document online. It quickly became apparent to them that not only Sasha's name was changed, but a lot of other children as well. If it wasn't for the test then many of them probably had no idea they were Crow famine adoptees and not adoptees in a more general sense. The thought made Amethyst very dizzy with stress.

Further inspection of the document revealed there wasn't a clear identification number that matched between the two documents and without original names of the adoptees then who knew who some of these children really were. The only way to know if they were Crow was to test them and nothing more. The irony that Amethyst wished she had testing data was not lost on her.

Many of the dates of when the adoption took place or rather was finalized were also missing. Birthdates didn't match between the two documents even with matching names and place of birth. Nearly everything was a mess. It became evident to Amethyst that this was probably on purpose. They never intended for any of this to be temporary. Or rather they were so messy about it because of the sheer number of adoptions that year. It was a six hundred percent increase over previous years.

"They didn't want to give anybody back. You know that," Sasha said, turning another page over.

Amethyst found her own name on the document, it was organized by date rather than first or last name.

"I was adopted twice. Maybe you were too?" Amethyst didn't know why she didn't think of this sooner.

"I was a toddler. I would remember if there was someone. I can barely remember..."

"What?" Amethyst pressed.

"No, nothing." Sasha flipped over another page.

"Don't do that."

"Do what?"

"Shut me out."

Amethyst couldn't read his mind and it bothered her, especially when they weren't communicating via speech.

"Just stop trying to read my mind" Sasha shook his head as if it would mentally shake Amethyst off.

Neither of them could explain how this was possible but as the days went on between them it seemed to get more normal and seem more natural. At first for Amethyst he was able to quiet his mind, she could hear his thoughts only softly but then he was able to fully shut her out.

"You have a habit of laying me bare, Amethyst"

Amethyst didn't respond immediately. She didn't know how to. She didn't know what exactly he meant by that.

"What do you mean by that?" Amethyst said, her voice soft at the end.

"I just mean you…you have a way of making me…I don't know. Forget it."

"No. I'm not gonna just forget it. What do you mean by that?"

"I don't know. I was just being foolish," Sasha said, closing the file.

Amethyst was going to say something else but feeling the stack of documents between the fingers of her right hand stopped the sentence in its tracks. They had so much they needed to do and digging around in Sasha's mind wasn't helping.

Amethyst glanced over the names on the list that were around his age. There was roughly 30. One of these were his actual name and if they could figure it out, they could fix everything.

UNWELL

Zora

Neither of them was well nor Zora couldn't help but to wonder what it would look like when the illness finally took them. Side by side on a full-sized bed on the second floor of the house they lay together. Eliza and her dad had broken out in a sweat that was unrelenting. Eric was sitting in the corner knitting away as if nothing was happening. It irritated Zora to no end. Did he not care about his brother?

But Zora, feeling the lack of her knowledge said nothing. Who really was she in the grand scheme of things. She didn't really know these people so who was she to judge? She felt like a foreigner in a foreign land. Even a place that was so common to her, the kitchen, was utterly alien to her. Half of the ingredients were in Crow.

"You can rest. It may take a while" Eric said as he scooped another loop off his needle, "I'll let you know if anything changes," he promised.

Zora nodded, not in agreement but robotically out of courtesy.

Eric looked up as he was making another stitch, and his eyes were glossy with tears.

Zora didn't say anything, but she simply watched as he made more stitches as he watched her. After an agonizing few moments Eric looked back down and continued making loops on his needles. Zora took this opportunity to leave the room. As she closed the door she heard a labored breath.

She was thankful that Eric didn't follow her and let her be.

In the kitchen Zora brewed herself a cup of coffee and sat at the kitchen island. She took each small mouthful of the hot liquid and let it live in her mouth for a second before drinking it down. Zora couldn't remember the last time she had a moment to herself. A moment without guests or prying questions. At the research compound, the hospital and now her parents home, Zora hadn't had many opportunities to simply be. But with this newfound freedom came the worry that she would miss something. She had never been on what could only be described as a death watch.

Eric was still up in the room, probably still knitting. Zora realized then she had never seen a man knit before watching Eric at work. He was doing beautiful work if she put away the circumstance in which he was doing it. He was working with a thin black yarn and white silvery yarn. Both looked incredibly soft.

Zora had her phone in her pocket and there was a part of her that wanted to take it out and text Muse but there was a bigger part that said now was not the time and Muse was probably dealing with the same thing this very moment.

Zora was able to ignore that voice though because she texted Muse.

How are you?

No response for a few minutes then:

. . .

Muse?

Suddenly three small dots appeared, ebbing and flowing to indicate typing.

I'm with them now. They're both really weak. I think it's started. Merit is with me.

This shattered Zora's heart and now her attention was squarely on Muse.

I'm so sorry.

The next thought Zora had was what kind of name was Merit and after a couple moments of searching Crow forums she discovered it was apparently a very popular name for Crow girls, especially Crow girls from Diamond Sea.

There was as lull in the conversation because Muse didn't text back for a full half hour.

How are you? I suppose bad. I mean, we did it around the same time. Oh, have you talked to Amethyst?

Zora hadn't text Amethyst since last night and she felt bad about that. But there was a part of her that just didn't want to have any proximity to Sasha. Even if it were all digital.

. . .

Zora texted back:

I haven't and yeah, my parents aren't well.

Zora didn't want to use the actual word and put that into the universe. There was something about it that made it feel all too final. Muse was thinking, the text bubble flashing the three dots again and another text appeared.

I'm not gonna lie to you anymore. I did think of Sasha. What happened was very confusing. I hope you're not upset. He didn't say you were an item just that you came over time to time.

The words stung but just to calm her nerves she took another sip of hot coffee. She found that it was now lukewarm. She texted back:

It's okay. We weren't together like that. Feel what you want to feel.

Zora regretted that last sentence but it was now too late to take it back. So she said;

I didn't mean to be so flippant about that. I just mean it's water under the bridge now.

It sounded better but not exactly what she wanted to say. It took a few minutes but Muse texted back.

Okay.

Zora knew then that she had fucked up big time and who knew if Muse would ever trust her with her thoughts ever again. There was no way for Zora to know this but it just felt like this was Muse's first crush. For it to be Sasha was such a heartbreaking thing. Sasha only cared about Sasha. He was selfish in so many ways. Emotionally. In the bedroom. Just so many ways. He was so incapable of truly loving anyone.

Zora put her phone face down on the kitchen island. Inside she knew if she kept talking to Muse that she would eventually launch into her like some rabid animal. She was angry that Muse didn't get it. Sasha's dad had called her a terrorist but Muse was still fine with Sasha because he seemed to make her panties wet.

She knew that if she had tried to explain just how Sasha was, she wouldn't be able to do it without crying. Where would she begin?

BABYSITTER

Muse

Merit hadn't left Muse alone for hours. After last night's tour of the house and this morning's rude awakening of both of her parents being ill, Merit seemed to be watching her like one would watch a tornado. Just silently waiting for her to either destroy everything in her path or break down and fade to nothingness.

Ava and who she knew now as David were in bed together and Muse couldn't bring herself to watch them like that. It was incredibly awkward to see them in bed together. They were as good as strangers to her. She felt bad for them but how one would feel bad for people in passing and not ones that she loved.

All the people she loved seemed to have abandoned her. She didn't tell Zora this, but she had her cell phone, and no one had texted her since she was arrested, not her mom, or Amethyst, and definitely not Sasha. Muse guessed the people at the research compound gave it back to her, but she didn't know how it was back in her possession. Muse hated not knowing things, especially when they concerned her. When Merit had finally left to go to the bathroom, Muse went to the guest room that was made up for her. It seemed to be all colors she disliked, burgundy and black. But the burgundy on closer inspection looked like a chocolate brown. Either way she hated it.

Merit had mentioned in passing that the name of the color was Maykis Burgundy, and she remembered learning about it in school, but this was her first time ever seeing the color in person. Depictions in books and on the news had the habit of looking much brighter than it did in real life.

The Maykis' were half owners of the company TerraTech, along with the Talis' family. Both were trillionaires. Both groups were incredibly dangerous people. There were rumors from a long time ago that they had parties where they traded and sold people. Nothing became of this rumor. No authority looked into it in the least. The rumors quickly died down on any website or paper. Comments talking about it on forums were mysteriously deleted, Including Muse's. Timothy Talis was recently in the news; people were speculating about him having a girlfriend and anytime these powerful men get a girlfriend or wife they somehow don't become more subdued but only get worse. It was like they were flexing their muscles.

Muse shook her head out of these thoughts because they were starting to distress her. It stressed her out more knowing that so many Crow men seemed to think the same way and she was now on their turf. Bluebird men weren't perfect either, but they didn't seem to play the same games as Crow men.

Amethyst had been in the territory for so long and Muse wondered if she ever was face to face with one. Would she have any real-life idea?

This is How it Ends

Zora

Zora's phone buzzed, moving slightly to the right on the kitchen island. She lifted it up. It was Eric telling her to come to the room. Zora texted back okay and went down the stairs to the bedroom. Eric meets her at the door. He held his hands out for her. Zora, confused, let her hands fall into his and Eric pulled her into the room. The sheet had been pulled over their heads and upon seeing this Zora backed away, nearly tripping over the extension cord that was coming from the heated throw on the bed.

She shook her head profusely and whispered something that even she couldn't discern what she said.

"It's okay, call the number that's on the yellow paper next to the fridge. They'll be able to locate our address and come for them."

Eric had avoided saying the word bodies, but Zora filled in the blanks for him. She bolted from the room, her whole-body quaking like a door in a windstorm.

In the kitchen the note was just where he said it would be, but Zora couldn't pick it up without trembling. She leaned against the kitchen counter and took a deep shaky breath before what she ate that morning began fighting its way up her throat. Zora's stomach violently lurched forward as she ran to the sink. She made it to the sink in time, but she would still have to clean it out later as none of it would go down the drain. Stomach now empty, she took a seat and tried to will herself to calm down. It was starting to feel painful, especially in her stomach.

Eric appeared, taking slow steady steps to her. He looked like he wanted to cry but his face was dry. He embraced Zora and she allowed him to. Nothing was said for a few minutes.

Eric had made the call for emergency services, and they waited for them to arrive at the kitchen table. He had made tea, and they were unsuccessfully attempting to drink it. It smelled like berries. It made Zora's mouth water, but she was unable to bring herself to think about the act of bringing it to her lips and not think about the fact that there were two bodies in the house.

OUT OF SIGHT, OUT OF MIND

Muse

Merit didn't let Muse see them after they had passed and instead told her to stay in the living area and wait for emergency services. They came ten minutes after they were called, and they immediately made their way up the stairs to the bedroom on the third floor.

Merit moved Muse again to the patio when they were making their way back down the stairs. Muse was grateful for this though she didn't say anything to Merit.

ARTIFACTS

Amethyst

The lawyer came back around again, knocking on the door and leaving another letter for Amethyst. This one was more detailed than the last one.

It was added:

This matter is of the utmost importance. Artifacts from your mother's life that have high monetary value are kept in a safe at our office. It is imperative that you get them at the earliest possible time:

City Center Complex East Quadrant 5900 Hart Avenue, Suite 2-B

Sasha and Amethyst then resolved to get them later that afternoon when Zircon returned from her date with the mystery man. For now, though they pawed through the rolls. Amethyst hadn't heard any thoughts from Sasha the entire time, even when he rested on the table, head down. He was getting better at keeping her out.

The patio was just as messy as the study, but it was the one place where they could get some fresh air and just breathe in the fresh air. After sitting there for about an hour, Amethyst could hear Zircon's thoughts first and then her car. She was focusing on her driving but underneath that was the thought of something else. She every now and then focused on the bracelet on her wrist. She parked in front of the house and walked in, hearing her own thoughts in Zircon's mind on top of her reading Zircon's mind created a layered unintelligible mess of sound.

Zircon came to the patio and took a seat in front of them. She shut Amethyst out then and observed the pair. Not seeming to like what she saw she sighed.

"Any luck?"

Amethyst and Sasha shook their heads and began stacking the paper together.

"You don't have to do all of that," Zircon said, looking up at the sky as if she was praying to a god.

"What's that?" Amethyst pointed to the bracelet on her wrist.

"To put it simply it acts as an engagement ring. Listen, we have a lot to talk about."

"You just started dating. I don't understand." Amethyst said, moving her chair closer to Zircon.

"We've known each other since we were kids," Zircon folded her hands in her lap.

"Well, who is he?"

"Timothy Talis."

The pair looked at each other, saying nothing at first but then looked back at Zircon who was now rubbing her thighs.

"We will make it official very soon." Zircon continued.

Ungodly

Sasha

Sasha knew the technology behind the bracelet, but he elected to say nothing to her. She probably already knew. That bracelet was outright illegal in the Bluebird Territory but in the Crow Territory there was a culture of using it. Especially among ultra rich couples. Zircon wore a decade of the average person's salary on her wrist. There was only one factory who made them, and they were a part of Maykis Industries. There was a part of Sasha that wished he were ignorant of what was going on between them. He would have to explain to Amethyst later. He didn't really know how but either way he did it would feel utterly invasive. It was the equivalent of having the 'talk' with a child.

Sasha nodded to Amethyst that they should go now to the office. Zircon agreed and they were on their way a few minutes later using Zircon's SUV. The drive was going to be a short one. They would drive to the train station and take it the rest of the way to the city center.

$\sim$

The drive to the city center was nice. The landscape was getting shorter and shorter revealing the pockets of beachfront properties. The air smelled salty and floral at the same time. When they came upon the station they parked in the lot and Sasha opened Amethyst's door. The pair of tickets were 24.32Z for the five stops they had.

The train ride would be roughly thirty minutes and Sasha elected to tell Amethyst just what was going on with Zircon. The train was heavily air conditioned. He could see his breath. Amethyst walked over to the middle of the train car so she could see the board with the LED lights that showed the status of the stops. Sasha sat next to her and wished they could've sat face to face.

"Amethyst," Sasha spoke softly, looking around to make sure no one was listening.

"Yeah," Amethyst said, still looking at the lights indicating the stops.

"We need to talk about your sister. About the bracelet she's wearing."

Amethyst didn't immediately look at Sasha. The expression on her face was one of "now what" and when her eyes finally rested on Sasha's there was a look of annoyance still within them.

"The bracelet she's wearing is more than just an indication that she's official with that guy. He can control the very pleasure center of her brain and turn it off on a whim. It's called a Laura bracelet. Named after the woman who designed it. Her version wasn't as powerful as the one Maykis Industries produces but the idea is still there. He controls her to a degree. It also tracks her movements. Do you know about the Talis family?"

Amethyst's eyes were laser focused on him now. She was trailing after every word. She shook her head yes. Her wavy hair bouncing a little.

"Good. They're up there with the Maykis, Snow, and lesser known Janis family. Timothy Talis is Luke Talis's younger brother."

"I didn't know he had a brother."

"He does and he's so much worse than Luke. He's really entrenched in high society and everything that comes with it. He doesn't necessarily want a girlfriend or a wife but someone who will keep up appearances to make him seem like he's a good person. Do charity and shit while he does horrible things for Maykis Industries."

Amethyst was considering his words, and her eyes were watering.

"Like your dad?"

"My dad didn't make my mom do anything she didn't want to," Sasha couldn't help the anger in his tone.

It had been a decade since she passed, and it was clear to him even then that she was in control. He always deferred to her when it came to what to do with him. Their relationship wasn't anything like it was between Timothy and Zircon.

"I meant doing dangerous things without any chance of answering for it," Amethyst corrected herself. Her tone had a finality to it.

"Zircon will be too busy to help us in any way. She'll be too busy— "Sasha stopped himself. He didn't want to get too graphic in his descriptions.

"Do you understand what I am saying?" Sasha asked.

"No, not really. I don't know why or how this bracelet is so important to everything."

"On the surface it's supposed to be a way to keep people from cheating and totally dependent on whoever wields it. It's not a normal amount of…it's ungodly."

Amethyst seemed to be considering his words now and the look that bloomed across her face was one of embarrassment. She was thinking about what he had said. His own words echoing back at him in his mind.

"Do you think Zircon knows all of this?" Amethyst finally said.

"I'm hundred percent sure that she knows. I wouldn't be surprised if your mom didn't plan this before she died or at the very least was hopeful it would happen."

There were three more stops, but Sasha wasn't sure if the conversation was done or not. He still wanted to say something about her comment, but he resisted. If he alienated her, then he was on his own in this strange territory.

The train came to a soft stop at City Center, and they disembarked. City Center looked ethereal in the afternoon, dressed in gold and pink light. They quickly found Hart Avenue and soon the east quadrant. It took them only a few minutes to get to the office. At the front was a young receptionist who gave Amethyst a form to fill out. It essentially stated that she was here to procure items related to Judy Millen upon her death. There were a lot of similar clipboards in a row behind the one the receptionist gave to her. Amethyst tried to count but the receptionist asked for them to take a seat. Amethyst couldn't help but to notice the bracelet on her wrist.

It was a while before anyone came for them. Sasha was on his cell phone and Amethyst was too. Sasha was too stressed to continue talking. He was wondering what these artifacts could be and all he could think about was jewelry or perhaps important papers.

An hour and twenty minutes later she was called in by a man with a large bald spot but contrasting young appearance. They were brought to a large room and on the table was a small cardboard box with a lid.

"This is everything related to your mother, the deed to the house etc etc. I just simply need you to sign your name next to each line as I show you each of the documents."

Amethyst nodded and walked up to the table.

"I'm sorry, I didn't introduce myself. I'm Mr. Grace. It's a pleasure to meet you Ms. Millen."

They shook hands and he swiftly began the process, taking each of the files out of the box and naming it before putting it back. It took about forty minutes. All Sasha could think of was it seemed like Amethyst was inheriting everything.

The ride back was noisy. It was the heat of rush hour; the train was full of people coming from work and school. In groups were children wearing school uniforms. Some of them held the hands of their parents. In Amethyst's mind Sasha could hear the ghost of his words in her head. Burning in her mind was who was this receptionist if she had a Laura bracelet like Zircon had.

"I don't know but she must be related to someone wealthy," Sasha said, answering her thought.

Amethyst pulled out her phone then and began texting. Sasha felt the vibration in his pocket. Amethyst had texted, *do you think Zircon is okay with this?*

Sasha thought back to her. *I don't really know. I think she's acting on obligation. She didn't look too comfortable even talking about it. It didn't seem like she was riding on cloud 9.*

Amethyst then thought back, *should I even say anything. I feel so out of place here.*

Sasha thought back then, *I would give her space for now.*

Back in the car they listened to the news:

A group of student protesters were arrested after painting the door of the immigration office in blue paint.

Sasha turned off the news then, feeling an all too familiar feeling well within his gut. One that made him feel guilty.

"You didn't know, Sasha," Amethyst answered. Sasha immediately shut his mind out. The rest of the drive was quiet. The only thing they both could hear was the sound of asphalt and rustling of trees in the strong wind. Amethyst thought about how odd it was that he had shut her out but she quickly turned to give him kindness. She thought he must be pretty traumatized from Ivy Ladder. Sasha knew he didn't deserve it.

TRIP

Zora

Eric had let her borrow the car. He filled the tank up completely and told her to drive safe. It was a twenty-minute drive to Muse's house and a five-hour drive to Diamond Sea. After Muse was picked up, they were on their way. Neither of them spoke for what seemed like forever. They sound of the radio softly playing traffic alerts being the only voice in the car. When they were halfway to their destination, they went into a bagel shop. It was down a narrow dirt road and inside a small house. Outside was a small grouping of tables and chairs, and all around the house's wrap-around porch were square tables and chairs in sets of two.

Inside were ladies dressed in petal pink maid outfits. Inside it was also really crowded. The smell inside made it clear why. Everything looked and smelled amazing.

Muse and Zora took a seat near the window, and they were quickly greeted by a maid with a booklet to take their order. They asked for a few minutes to get their thoughts together and she left to seat another pair.

Muse looked out the window, folding her arms on top of the table. Muse didn't hear Zora trying to talk to her. She didn't even look at the menu that was underneath her arms.

Zora decided on a bagel with butter and an ice-cold brew. She was tempted to order a coffee for Muse as well, but she decided she would wait for her to come back down to Earth. She didn't have to wait for long because Muse looked her directly in the eyes at that moment and asked if she could ask her a question.

Zora nodded yes and expected it to be something light and simple like what she was gonna order or something like that.

"Do you believe in heaven?"

Zora was taken aback by her question, and she felt a little nervous behind it as well.

"I guess I believe we all go somewhere but I'm not sure in heaven in the sense of as a reward" Zora flipped over the menu, trying to stop the conversation in its tracks.

"Oh, okay." Muse looked back out the window and then quickly returned her gaze to the inside of the cafe when she heard the click of heels coming toward them. She scanned the menu.

Zora felt like shit at that moment. What kind of friend was she? She should've lied but now it was too late. When the maid came over Muse ordered first, a large latte and a plain donut and a side of cheesy eggs. Zora ordered then, surprised that Muse was able to formulate what she wanted so quickly.

"How did you order so fast?" Zora asked when the maid was out of earshot.

"I just listened to what other people seemed to be ordering the most and ordered the same," Muse said, not looking at Zora. She looked as though she might tear up but she didn't.

"I'm sorry," Zora said.

"What are you apologizing for?" Muse looked confused.

"Nothing. Nothing."

~

In the car Muse went to the back seat and took a nap as Zora drove. Zora was relieved she didn't have to have any conversation. She didn't know what she would say to Muse. She knew she was fighting with her own grief monster and Zora had yet to content with hers. All she felt was numb. She didn't even feel the fabric of the car seat on her skin. Everything was numb including touch.

Muse softly snored before long and for a while it was the only constant sound in the large SUV. Every now and then Zora would turn on the radio and scan for stations, hoping to hear a familiar song or news that wasn't about protest and President Luke Talis, but she was shit out of luck on that front. The President of the territory was issuing a warning to Snow to return the remainder of the "Lost Children" or face consequences. Zora didn't listen to the news long enough to have what he meant by consequences explained. She didn't want to imagine what it could mean. It was the Crow Territory and as a toddler Zora knew about how they pushed the Eagle further into the corner of the map. It was ugly.

Muse was driving now, and Zora sat in the passenger seat. Muse was a good driver despite not having as many opportunities to drive. She glided from one area to the next. It was like it was second nature to her. The sun had already set, and the trees were castling long shadows on the hood of the car.

"Where did you learn to drive?"

"Mostly from my dad. My mom was used to being driven around. I wouldn't trust her to teach me much of anything having to do with heavy machinery."

"Ah, I see," Zora couldn't help but to laugh. It didn't feel like a natural laugh. It almost felt nervous. She couldn't understand why. She knew Muse for years.

"You, okay?" Muse said.

She seemed to notice and that further put Zora on edge.

"Not really. I'm just really nervous right now. I don't know why." Zora said as she sat up more in her seat.

"Really? You can't imagine why? You're going into the belly of the beast. You're gonna be face to face with Sasha."

"No, I've made peace with that," Zora said, watching the road.

"Have you really? It doesn't really seem like it from here," Muse said.

The question irritated Zora's nerves, but she quieted them and just nodded yes.

"It's okay. You feel how you feel about him."

"And you don't?" Zora implored.

"I was confused but I'm not...no. That's not right, he doesn't make me feel uncomfortable," Muse said, seemingly thinking out loud.

"You should," Zora said, mostly to herself.

Muse laughed then, loudly. There was almost a hint of anger behind the laugh like she was done with Zora and Zora couldn't ignore it.

"Your feelings are not the be all and end all. Not everyone has to feel the way you do," Muse said, making a turn. A dark smile came across her face, in what little light that was left, Zora could barely make out the rest of her face. She was just a smile. A large, blindingly white smile.

"He was never in danger. Ever. He was never arrested. Never questioned," Zora said, not looking Muse in the face.

"And you think it's because what?" Muse asked, gently careening on the side of a street to park.

"He was a plant," Zora said flatly.

"The whole time? That's what you think?" Muse's voice gentle now. The cruel feature to her voice gone now.

"I don't know. I have no proof I just— "Zora stopped herself.

"You want him to suffer like you did. That's really kind coming from someone who's supposed to be his girlfriend," Muse said this matter of factly.

"He's not my fucking boyfriend," Zora was angry now and she spat the last word at Muse. Muse was still holding on to the steering wheel, her knuckles white now. Muse shook her head now. She said nothing. Zora regretted even participating in this conversation. She couldn't convince Muse. There was something underneath her words that she wasn't letting up on. Zora had feelings for Sasha but it was complicated. Why did Muse take so much offense to her distrust? What would be gained if she continued the fantasy that Sasha couldn't possibly be blamed for anything? Zora also didn't understand why this conversation kept being had. Before Ivy Ladder Zora tried to convince her then and now it seemed like every other business month, she had to convince her that Sasha was dangerous.

"We're here." Muse said, breaking Zora out of her rotating thoughts.

～

It was a short walk up a hill and down the path to Amethyst's sister's house. The light was on on the first floor and dark everywhere else. Zora texted Zircon that they were here, and they were let in by her. By the smell and by the heat Zora could tell that Zircon was cooking something in the kitchen.

"Amethyst and Sasha were sitting out on the patio" Zircon said, answering Zora's thoughts.

They both made their way through the living room and out of the small door that led to the patio. Amethyst and Sasha were right next to each other talking quietly when they arrived. Zora had never seen them like this before. They were friends for much longer than Zora was with them, but this was the first time she had ever seen them sitting so… close.

Sasha didn't look all that excited to see Zora. He looked at her like he couldn't believe she was standing in front of him.

Amethyst got up and embraced them both, squashing them into each other.

"It's so good to see you guys," Amethyst said, still holding them hostage.

Zora looked at Muse and was relieved to see her features had softened. Amethyst let go, she still was smiling.

"It's good to see you too," Muse said.

Zora mumbled the same.

. . .

The group sat around the patio table,very few words exchanged between them. It was mostly Amethyst who talked, just sharing her excitement that they were safe. No one said the quiet part out loud about what it truly meant that they were safe. It had only been roughly a week since Zora and Muse's parents had passed. Amethyst looked tired to Zora. Like she hadn't slept well in days.

"How are you, Amie?" Muse said.

Amethyst seemed to be caught off guard and smiled, which quickly fell from her face.

"I'm okay," She softly replied.

In the kitchen Muse and Sasha ended up seated together and Zora was very curious if Muse liked the arrangement or not. Muse's face was blank as she watched for her reaction when it happened. Amethyst helped Zircon set the place settings and ladle soup into bowls. Zora's mouth watered.

They ate at first mostly in silence. There was a periodic comment on the weather or the news, but it was mostly quiet. Everyone seemed tired and hungry.

The group migrated to the living room and Zircon let them be. She retired to her bedroom to sleep.

"If you're tired, I can show you guys to your rooms," Amethyst said.

"That'd be great actually," Zora piped up.

SOCIETY

Muse

She was glad Zora was gone. The question she wanted to ask was burning deep inside of her. The maid in the cafe and now on Amethyst's sister was that bracelet that Merit refused to talk about. When Amethyst went up to show Zora her room, Muse broached the subject to Sasha.

"Hey," Muse began, sitting closer to him. He seemed to be the same old Sasha. His emerald green eyes seemed to soften when he looked up at her, but she couldn't be sure of that.

"What's up?"

"I don't know how to bring this up. I tried asking my maid and she wouldn't explain it to me."

"What?" Sasha looked curious.

"Do you know what that bracelet is that Zircon is wearing?"

Sasha looked down for a moment before looking back up to her. His eyes are slightly wider than before.

"I do know what it is. It's a Laura bracelet."

"But what does it do?"

Sasha gently took her hand in his.

"I don't know if you're...it's a tool. Mostly for the elites. Usually used between couples"

This utterly confused Muse because if it were usually couples, then why would the maid have one? Who's her other half? Sasha's eyes became even wider then.

"What?"

"You said your maid?"

"Yes, my maid wore one, but she wouldn't tell me what it did."

"Muse, sorry if this question is a bit invasive but were your parents' wealthy?"

"I'd say so, yes. Merit told me my dad worked for Maykis Industries."

"Oh," Sasha nodded yes and then looked away momentarily before looking back. Muse could sense he was avoiding saying what he really meant.

"Can you just spit it out?" Muse demanded.

"Your maid isn't just a maid. She was probably sleeping with your dad. Or your mom. Or both. Who really knows," Sasha didn't look at Muse when he said any of this.

"That's disgusting. Why would you say any of that?"

Amethyst was standing in the doorway to the living room. Muse didn't know how long she had been there.

"Is everything?" Amethyst started, before taking a seat across from the pair.

"No, nothing is alright. Sasha just accused my dad of cheating on my mom. They haven't even been in the ground a week" Muse looked up at Amethyst.

"Aren't you going to say anything?" Muse continued.

"I don't know if any of that is true, but I do know the purpose of that bracelet and how expensive it is. It's not all that farfetched to put two and—

"No," Muse put up her hand as if to halt the conversation.

The conversation ended there, and Muse walked up the staircase. To do what, she didn't know. She just knew she had to be out of that room that was beginning to feel all too suffocating.

OLD BRANCH

Zircon

The entire conversation was in her head, echoing off every wall of her brain like an empty room. She felt bad for Muse, that she had to have found out this way but anyone who was anyone knew that the Janis family often bought prisoners for servitude. Muse was a Janis and this reputation would follow her. She would've found out eventually. It was better she was finding out from a friend and not a stranger on the street. Especially not from a stranger that opposed what some elite families did.

Zircon went out into the hall and saw Muse sitting at the top of the stairs, leaning against the right side of the stairs. Muse didn't acknowledge her presence until she was right behind her.

"The Janis family, your family. Is a lot like the Millen family, my family. An old branch. And sometimes they have to do certain things to keep up their reputation. Some of it good and some of it questionable. It's the culture of this place. It's really complicated. If you want to talk about it I'm here," Zircon said. She could see how Muse's eyes were blurry with tears.

"What's an old branch?"

"Someone who can trace their lineage back many generations, often to the first families to ever populate the island. And of course the families who were a part of the first judicial body, The Night Crows."

"The old branches are dying out. The new branches are taking over," Zircon said as she took a seat beside Muse.

Muse looked up then. Her hazel eyes lacked focus. She looked utterly exhausted.

"Like keeping slaves," Muse said.

"You can't use that word in public, especially not among the elites. You don't want to alienate yourself."

"Why would I want to be among people who would do something so monstrous?" Muse's eyes were hard now.

"Those rumors of parties and selling people were true then?" Muse spoke more to herself than to Zircon.

"Those people were either criminals or—"

"They signed up for it?" Muse finished.

"Yes," Zircon said.

"And there was no possibility of them being coerced into it?" Muse continued.

"I don't know the contents of every one's mind—"

"I don't believe you," Muse said, head to the ceiling. Muse wiped her face but the tears continued to come.

"The money your parents left you will run out at a certain point. If you want to create anything for yourself, you have to play the game." Zircon touched Muse on her shoulder. Muse shook her off.

"I'd tell my sister the same thing if she were in your predicament," Zircon said firmly.

"That's supposed to make me feel grateful to you?"

"It's the reality of the situation," Zircon lifted Muse's chin up.

Muse was about to say something, but she resisted once she saw the grave look in Zircon's storm cloud gray eyes.

JANIS FAMILY

Sasha

He didn't know much about the Janis family apart from the Janis family had a large contract with TerraTech. For what, he didn't know. Usually for wealthy people it was security. They were probably securing the maid. Though Sasha didn't know the exact number, he knew the number for a prisoners' contract was a ridiculous sum of money. Especially one that was for personal use like Muse's maid. Sasha knew Amethyst would hear all of this and that was the point. He wasn't in the mood to actually talk but he needed someone else to know.

"How do you know all of this?" Amethyst said.

My dad rubbed elbows with a lot of these people. He thought it was important for me to know how they think. What they value.

In his mind's eye he could still see Muse at the top of the stairs with Zircon. Zora was out of her room and watching them. She had heard most of the conversation and she surprisingly wasn't as judgmental as he was expecting. She felt bad for Muse. Zora left the hallway before Zircon and Muse got up from the stairs. Sasha guessed she didn't want to be a part of the cleaning up the fallout from any breakdown that

Muse might have. It was not every day that one found out their parents enslaved people.

"What kind of crimes lead to—"Amethyst trailed off.

So many kinds. Chewing gum and walking at the same time. Anything they decide.

"Who's they?"

Whoever is the best at lobbying.

Amethyst unsteady got up from the armchair and sat directly next to Sasha, looking into his eyes, perhaps she wanted to see if what he was saying was the truth.

Tell me more about this, Amethyst plopped this thought into his head.

He pulled the curtain to his mind then. He knew way more than he was comfortable sharing with her.

"Why'd you do that?" Amethyst looked confused.

"Some things are just too dark. I'll tell you some of what I know but maybe the rest later."

Just think them. I already don't think all that highly of them anyway.

Sasha thought immediately how ironic it was because she was one of them, whether she considered herself one or not. He forgot to keep shutting her out and she heard this thought.

"I'm not like them!" Amethyst sounded half offended and half surprised that he would think that.

Catastrophe

Zora

Zora's mind was spinning. She nearly walked into the dresser that was beside the doorway as she walked in. She was grateful for the adjoining bathroom because she felt sick. Nothing came up. Everything was already deep in her digestive system.

She sat at the edge of the bathtub and couldn't help but to think about what Muse said about the parties and how at these parties' people were bought. It made no difference if they were criminals. They were still human beings. She would have to ask later how she knew about these parties. Her family was in the suburbs, who knew what her parents did. At least Zora knew what her mom did and didn't hide that fact.

Zora heard a low vibration, almost like a hum. She took out her cell phone and saw an alert on her phone that everyone in Diamond Sea is to shelter in place. No other details were revealed.

Immediately after, she heard a knock on the bathroom door. It was Muse, she knew those footfalls anywhere. Zora realized she didn't close the bedroom door.

"Turn on the news," Her voice was strained. She sounded like she was about to cry.

Zora steeled herself for whatever this might be. She turned flipped through pages of apps until she landed on the news app and in a large flashing yellow square it said, "Falling Catastrophe in Diamond Sea". She clicked on it and immediately wished she had not. Filling her eyes were horrifying videos and pictures of young people splayed out on the pavement. It didn't make any sense whatsoever. They were already in the territory. Their parents probably already transferred their power to them. Why were they sick?

"Did you see it, oh god, why is this happening?" Muse opened the door. She didn't look anything but exhausted.

"Maybe they didn't do the ceremony," Zora sounded hopeful even to herself.

"Some of them just did it. It doesn't make any sense," Muse corrected her.

"It all seems random," Muse added.

Zircon entered the room, taking pointed strides to the bathroom.

"You guys feel fine?"

The pair nodded yes. Zircon sighed then sat next to Zora on the tub.

"Some of them were recently changed. I have never seen anything like this in my life. In The Falling, all of those kids weren't changed at all. They were long overdue." Zircon looked as though she was trying to be careful with her words. April 4th was a date that was seared into her mind. Each year after that it passed Zora would get depressed. Even when she lost track of the days. It was like her body knew.

Zircon got up from the tub and just left the small bathroom, Muse trailing behind her.

Preventative Measures

Amethyst

It all felt like it was all for naught. If the ceremony couldn't prevent another Falling, then what could? Sasha was intently listening to her thoughts. Responding to them with his eyes. Sasha was distressed too and Amethyst could discern that from the cadence of his thoughts. Like a video, all the protests that he had participated in played in her mind. Sasha felt guilty. He felt as though he had caused all of this by spreading the idea that the "Lost Children" should stay within the Bluebird Territory. He shut her out then. Head hanging down, a few tears escaped.

"None of us knew. But we know now and it's what we do with that information now that truly matters."

Sasha was trembling now and Amethyst wanting to comfort him was about to touch his shoulder, but he jerked up and stood out of reach.

Zora appeared then at the bottom of the staircase with Muse and Zircon. The look on Muse's face was grave. She looked as though she had narrowly escaped death. Amethyst thought perhaps they in actuality did. Who knew how this falling worked. Perhaps it was truly random, and it could have been any of them. Sasha hearing her thoughts walked closer to the group and spoke softly, "I think we should go to bed and deal with this in the morning."

"Not a big enough deal to deal with it now, huh?" Zora spat.

Sasha groaned, "I'm tired. You're tired. Nothing will get done any faster if we're sleep deprived." He mostly spoke this to Zora who looked on with a disgusted look on her face. She folded her arms, her hands half trembling as she did this. She looked as though she vibrated with anger. Sasha didn't look phased.

"Hey, we will deal with this tomorrow. Nothing can be done now. We wouldn't even be able to look up who these people are without names. How are we gonna start our research with just hearsay?" Amethyst said as she strode closer to Zora.

Zora looked as though there was more, she wanted to say but she resisted and went up the stairs, Muse followed her. Zircon stayed. She didn't say anything, but it was clear from her facial expressions that a lot was heavy on her mind.

"In the morning," she seemed to say more to herself than Amethyst or Sasha and she went up the stairs.

～

The morning crashed into being. The sun rays blazing through her eyelids. It couldn't have been six hours, but it was and now the side table clock was reading 8:03 in angry red numbers. Sasha was at her door then, lightly knocking. She could see from his mind's eye the other side of the door.

They trickled into the kitchen one by one. Muse helped herself to some cereal, Zora was making eggs for everyone, and Sasha and Amethyst had mugs of coffee. Zircon was out on the patio taking a call. Amethyst could only hear half of the conversation. Zircon had shut her out. She was done in hardly any time, and she joined everyone else in the kitchen. With her she brought some papers. They were all freshly printed off and still warm to the touch.

Sasha was the first to read anything. Each first column had a name, the second had an age and the last one had a location. It was every person who had fallen last night. The final tally was a hundred and one. Far more than the first falling. The initial fall was twenty-eight. The average age was twenty-one and all the locations were Diamond Sea. It was like some kind of bomb went off and only affected that area and nowhere else. It was strange. Like the falling on April 4th, all the young people had suffocated and died on the spot. It was like a horror movie. TerraTech of course was looking into it as well but what in actuality could they do about it if they knew nothing about the Crow territory's secrets? How much help would they actually be? Amethyst tried her best not to focus on that and instead turned her attention back to the stack of paper that Zircon had printed off. The other roll of names was easy to miss because it was so short and it showed the various locations that it happened, Goose Grasshopper Lane, Bluebird stream, Clayton and more. It was primarily concentrated in the Bluebird Territory, which was no surprise to anyone.

"Where did you get this?"

"Internal database don't worry about it,"Zircon said as Amethyst turned to another page.

"Did Timothy give you this?"

Zircon didn't answer immediately but sighing she nodded and looked Amethyst into the eyes.

There wasn't a lot that could be inferred from the information Zircon gave them, so the group had breakfast and retired into the living room. Zora was more subdued and didn't look as angry as she looked before at Sasha. Amethyst really couldn't understand why. They protested together. Did the grassroots things together. It really didn't make sense to her why she was angry with Sasha. Maybe she felt like Sasha was spending too much time with her. Maybe that was it. But even that didn't seem proportional to her anger. Amethyst decided then the next time she was alone with Zora she would ask that very question. For a moment she thought about reading her mind, but she thought that would be too intrusive, so she changed her mind.

The news wasn't helpful. It was maddening. It looped saying the same thing, that they didn't know what was happening and names were coming out and they're trying to maintain calm. The only real updated information was they blocked off some streets so they could essentially collect the adults who had fallen. No one knew and for Amethyst it seemed like no one really cared to know and they had wholesale accepted that this was a normal part of life. Bluebird or Crow news, it didn't matter. The sound of worry was at the same decibel.

Zircon turned off the news then and called her boyfriend again as asked him if he knew anything new. He didn't.

Later that night it was only Amethyst and her imagination. Despite not knowing much of anything she could guess at what she thought was happening. There were no rules against that. Though the list of who was changed and who was not was not public knowledge, Muse was able to use her skills combing through message boards to find out if any of the names matched with those who were lost children who had recently made a visit to a certain pond. This information was outright illegal to collect but anyone who needed to know wasn't doing what was right by that information anyway. Only a few names overlapped. The rest was anyone's guess.

WHERE THE LIGHT SHINES

Zora

She wished she could zap herself out of existence. Muse trailing behind her like a puppy and Sasha breathing in her direction, it was all too much. Amethyst and Sasha seemed to develop a bit of a relationship before they parted ways, and it confused her. They were friends, much longer than they were together but Amethyst hung around Sasha like the light shines from his ass. When she thought that she couldn't help but to notice Sasha smiled.

Her thoughts were interrupted by another emergency alert on her phone. She held her breath to see that another falling had occurred. They all did. But the alert read: *Normal activity and traffic can resume.*

"Oh, thank god," Muse said, her voice wavering.

"Why thank God? It was bound to happen?" Zircon said.

"I am just grateful that…never mind. It's stupid," Muse stood up then and walked into the kitchen. Zora was glad she had some breathing room back.

Amethyst was scrolling on her phone then, it looked like a news app. She slid to a couple of articles before turning off her phone screen.

"How have you been, Amethyst," Zora moved closer to the armchair that Amethyst was sitting on.

"Fine," Amethyst said, not even bothering to look up.

Zora said nothing more and got up to head towards the kitchen. She didn't understand the change in Amethyst attitude, and she wasn't going to sit there and be stuck in it. She would make herself a cup of tea and come back to it later.

Can we talk about that day?

Muse

Muse was thinking similarly, and she made herself some coffee and retired to the patio. When Zora joined her, Muse took the opportunity to try to talk to her.

"Hi," Muse said into her cup, she then looked up as she tried to smile to be friendly.

"Hey," Zora responded, placing her mug on the wicker table in front of them, and taking a seat.

"I just wanted to apologize for how I acted in the car. I don't know what came over me."

"*What came over you?*" Zora repeated as she took a sip of her tea.

"Yeah. I just couldn't accept that he would *use* me like that."

"I tried to explain this to you," Zora not realizing how harsh this sounded but she continued, "he does this to everyone."

"How much do you think he says is true?" Muse was looking at every expression on Zora's face.

"I don't imagine a lot."

Muse nodded then and took another sip of her coffee. The sun was now high in the sky, cresting over the trees. From their vantage point they could see a flower garden, further still, trees and further than that a pond. The look of the pond made Muse internally shake.

"Can we talk about that day?" Muse had to get some clarity.

"Ivy Ladder?"

"Yeah."

"What about it?"

"Why do you think he did what he did?" Muse rubbed her fingers over the side of the cup, collecting the moistened warmth that lived there.

"He probably thought he could get you to change your mind by kissing you. He was trying to seduce you. That's all."

Muse didn't like the answer, but she was sure Zora was right. He was trying to influence her decisions. Muse just didn't like the word seduce. It made her feel like an object. The conversation seemed to dry up then because the pair just sat there and had their hot drinks in silence. In Muse's mind she could still hear the word seduce bounce around her head like a hard rubber ball.

Everyone was called to the living room at noon. Muse was not looking forward to facing whatever was going on. She already had to contend with the fact that her parents owned a person and an illness that was killing people her age on top of that was just too much.

Amethyst and Sasha were standing in front of the mantel about to talk. Zora had her arms folded and Zircon was setting out sandwiches she made that were wrapped in parchment paper. Muse didn't have an appetite. All she felt was constantly parched and all she wanted to do was drink.Sasha looked at Muse then and then averted his gaze to rest on Zora.

"What?" Zora said.

Sasha shook his head and cleared his throat.

"There are some things you guys should know. Amethyst and I are related in some way. We don't know how. But she was able to perform the ritual in the pond and transfer some of her power to me. I'm now what eve calls "Half-Blessed" meaning the process is not complete because she's not my mom. We have been trying to figure out who I am, but my name was changed after I was adopted. Perhaps having more eyes on this you guys can help us figure out who I really am."

"Half-blessed?" Zora was really paying attention now, she untwined her arms and sat at the edge of the chair.

"Yes," Sasha said.

"My dad was "half-blessed "; he never was able to figure out a way to undo it. It left him susceptible to human illness. Women who do the ceremony become a dead end. They can't have children. Men who do it can potentially become ill and die," Zora spoke these matter-of-factly.

Zircon was looking intently at Zora now, processing her words. She walked out of the room then and went into the kitchen. After a few moments there was a loud scream that floated from the kitchen and deep in their eardrums. Amethyst looked as though she just woke up from a terrible nightmare. Amethyst looked even more distressed then and Sasha, seeming to sense this, stood close to her. She nearly collapsed but he caught her in his arms. Muse stood up then and walked over to them. She helped Sasha sit Amethyst on the couch.

A few minutes later Zircon reappeared, her face was streaked with tears.

"I'm so sorry. I'm so sorry. I'm so sorry," Amethyst repeated herself. She looked like she was in a trance.

"We're done. I can't believe this," Zircon said into her hands, tears dripping down from her cupped hands.

"Wh—what do you mean?" Amethyst stammered.

"Our family line is over. A five hundred years, just gone."

"She's the only one?" Muse tried her best to be careful with her words but even that short sentence sounded so harsh to her.

"Yes," Zircon whispered.

Muse couldn't stay in the living room. She left for the bathroom. Saying as such as she left. In the bathroom she took a couple of measured breaths. A cry erupted from her throat. One she wasn't expecting. This fucking magic was life ruining, and she wanted no part of it. But she knew she was stuck living with this magic in her veins, doomed to die to transfer it to another. And it could only be her. There was no way around her continuing the family line herself. Muse didn't want a baby. She barely could take care of herself and keep herself out of trouble. How could she do the same for a whole other person? She sat at the edge of the tub. Trying to keep down the drink she had earlier that morning. In spite of everything else that was going on she was grateful that what was happening between Amethyst and Sasha could not in any stretch of the imagination ever become romantic. They were related and this knowledge made her feel better. It meant that Amethyst wasn't under his influence. Muse didn't go back into the living room until nearly an hour later. By that time everyone was spread about the house. Zircon was back in her room according to Zora and Sasha and Amethyst were in their rooms.

Muse took a seat next to Zora and just sat back, grateful for the quiet company. Zora turned to her then, "should I have not said anything?" she whispered.

"No. They should know. You didn't do anything wrong."

"I wish my dad was still alive. I can't ask him what he tried and what didn't work."

"I wish my parents were still alive. At least you get to go back to your uncle. I have to go back to the maid my parent's owned."

Muse thought about the big empty mansion she would have to go back to and the thought made her feel incredibly empty.

"I'm sorry, Muse. I really am," Zora said as she sat up more.

"You don't have to apologize. Such is life," Muse swept her arm across the room.

"You could come stay with me. There's no law saying you have to stay in that house."

"I'm sure there is," Muse wasn't going to get her hopes up.

Muse regretted declining the invitation outright. She liked the idea of staying with Zora but her heart couldn't bare another disappointment.

DEAD END

Amethyst

Zircon had not stopped crying. She didn't let Amethyst in her mind either. She was keeping these walls up with great difficulty because here and there she could hear a fleeting word or pictures from a disjointed thought. Amethyst felt an immense amount of guilt. She didn't know but it didn't matter because the result was, she was throwing away half a millennium of her family's line if she didn't find a way to make Sasha no longer "Half-Blessed".

A break in the crying led to Amethyst seeing Zircon walking over to her cell phone. A number and name flashed across her thoughts before all Amethyst saw was darkness. She was gonna talk to Timothy.

She decided to focus on herself then. She took a deep breath and walked toward the adjoining bathroom to take a shower. She hadn't showered yet and she was beginning to smell the sweat from last night.

~

Zircon traveled the house like a ghost for the rest of day. Amethyst could see her talking to Timothy and she tried her best to not listen. One detail that she couldn't ignore was Zircon taking a picture of her

Laura bracelet for her socials. It was happening. She was making it official. When she uploaded the picture, she turned off her notifications. The thinking behind that was the post would go viral and she wouldn't be able to keep up with the constant song of pings.

It was only a few moments, but the silent pings happened. It was like a waterfall across the screen. One by one they popped up and then were shuffled underneath the other notifications to make room for the next one. Zircon's thoughts seemed to quiet then, she sighed.

LITTLE SISTER

Sasha

Sasha could see everything happening in the kitchen. He was thankful that Zircon and Talis were going to go official, knowing that the Millen family line was going to end. She deserved her happily ever after. Whatever form that was going to take.

He spent the very bulk of the afternoon reading Zora's mind and every curse she was yelling in her head about him. There was confusion there too. She couldn't understand why he and Amethyst were so close. She put it out of her mind that they were romantically involved. She sensed and was right that there was something more. Amethyst and Sasha decided to keep their mind reading a secret for now. Zircon had agreed. It wasn't uncommon for families with certain gifts to keep those gifts a secret to those outside of the family line. The secrecy of powers had certain advantages. Zora and Muse hadn't mentioned anything about having a gift and it made him wonder if that was the case for them as well. Or their parents didn't tell them and left them to figure it out themselves. According to Zircon the latter wasn't uncommon. If anything it was more traditional. She answered his thought from the other room.Sasha was grateful for Zircon. He wouldn't have been able to make this decision without her input. She knew about the social aspects of their world.

In the middle of his thoughts he was distracted by Muse. She was thinking about Ivy Ladder for the fifth time today. Dissecting every scene one by one. He kissed her and he should've but watching it on constant loop was beginning to make him angry. He had to do it or she was going to shatter an entire multi-ton pane of glass on hundreds of people. People would've died if it hadn't been for him. Her mind began to float to the Maykis Statue fiasco. She didn't think about that for long. Her stomach interfered with her thoughts, making her think of grabbing one of the last few sandwiches and some ice tea instead of thinking about the protest.

Amethyst was also calling him in her thoughts so he left his room for hers.

~

She was laying on her bed, looking up at the ceiling. She wasn't thinking of much. He was about to ask why he had called her when she said, "do you think I'm really a dead end or would trying to have kids end in some other kind of disaster? Like the kid would be human and not have any magic?", she sighed and continued, "I guess that would really mean a dead end, wouldn't it?"

"Well, there's no way to test your theory?"

Amethyst looked at Sasha with a smirk.

"No real way right now, especially without time and a person," Sasha said.

Amethyst rummaged around in his head and found a morsel of a thought about babies taking multiple tries to make and that doesn't even account for the gestation.

"Why would anyone want to try with me, being a dead end and all anyhow. Did you see what Zircon did this morning?" Amethyst added.

"I did."

"And?"

"And what? I'm glad she's happy. She deserves it. If she's going to put some kind of honor on your family name, aligning with Talis would definitely give her points, don't ya think?"

"I think he must know what TerraTech is doing to lost children too. Has to be some useful information. Do you think we'd be able to talk to him about it?" Amethyst half sat up, her elbows keeping her at an angle.

"That's Zircon's contact. I don't think she'd let us. The information he's sharing has got to be classified," Sasha said.

"But he's practically family. Maybe he'd give us a little bit of information," Amethyst sounded a little more hopeful now.

"I don't know…" Sasha trailed off.

There was no way of stopping her because as soon as half a beat passed she was up on her feet and on her way towards Zircon. Zircon was now sitting on the patio, responding to her post concerning her engagement to Talis. Amethyst wasted no time when she got there and she asked in as sweet a way as possible did she think Timothy would know more about the falling and potentially Sasha's background.

Zircon didn't look up and only nodded.

"I already asked for his help. He's the one who gave me the list of who fell. I'm waiting for more information."

"Oh."

"Yeah. Little sister, of course I would ask on your behalf. Give me a little more credit," Zircon said as she began typing another comment.

CONNECTIONS

Amethyst

Zircon expected an email, a text message, not reams of paper delivered to her address. There were three boxes. She shook her head as she looked inside the document boxes. Each one of them in alphabetical order. The first box was adoption papers for every lost child that was adopted around the same time as Sasha, the second box was about the TerraTech Turpeek research and the last box was the family trees of the major six families, Maykis, Talis, Snow, Janis, Clover and Millen. The first three, all new branches, the second three, all old branches.

"Do you think they're gonna notice all of this missing?" Amethyst said.

"Probably not. These are all copies of the originals."

"He did all this?" Sasha said.

"His secretary most likely did it," Zircon said as she opened another one of the boxes.

"Yeah, that makes sense but still this is so much. I can't thank him enough," Amethyst said, taking out the first file she laid her eyes on.

"I'll be sure to tell him," Zircon said.

Zora and Muse had gotten a hotel a few miles away near City Center wanting some more space. The trio knew from what, though they said nothing about it. Amethyst knew that the protesting got messy sometimes so she hadn't pressed Sasha but she kept her thoughts at bay because she didn't want to know more than she bargained for. She already knew about how Sasha betrayed Zora by kissing Muse. And betrayed Muse by trying to seduce her out of committing a terrorist attack. It was all already too much to know. Occasionally when she was tired these thoughts would surface and Sasha would hear them but he seemed to be ignoring them.

Amethyst looked at the file she took out. It was a list of participants, phase I, dated for last year. A lot of it went over her head. She couldn't understand the data. She glanced over the names and recognized the little cross beside them, indicating death. 2/3rd of them had died. She quickly closed the file and looked at the one that was next, Phase II. There were better odds for them, only half had died. Phase III, there was very little data, but there was a note it was still ongoing. She saw two names that she recognized, Zora Jo'nest and Muse Ophilla Drew. She then flipped to the back of the paper, it was a chart showing the amounts of Cerplex along with the heart rates of the participants. As the amount of Cerplex was increased, the heart rate and other vital signs slowed but outward appearance would have one believe they were healthy.

"Come look at this, now," Amethyst's tone was commanding. The rest of the group looked over her shoulder to read the study.

"They're dosing those kids with Cerplex?" Zircon's tone was one of utter disgust.

"Yeah," Sasha's voice contrasted with Zircon's. While hers' was half shock, half surprised, Sasha's was matter-of-fact mixed with something else Amethyst couldn't name.

"Did you know about this, Sasha?" Zircon was careful with her words because she was thinking of a more inappropriate string of words to say.

"My dad was treating the illness in me with Cerplex. I didn't know he was doing it to other people too."

"That sounds a lot like child abuse," Zircon was less choosy with her words in that instance.

"It helped me. It kept me alive for all this time," Sasha felt defensive, there was a row of comebacks he had for both of them.

"How are you so sure?" Zircon spoke carefully.

"He ran a test, discovered the gene was greatly suppressed in my DNA. I haven't had any episodes of pain since he started using Cerplex."

Amethyst had nothing to say. Zircon's mind was also blank.

"I know what he did was really unorthodox but he didn't know what he was doing and what he was doing was helping some people."

"They should've gone back with their families. They shouldn't have been being tested on like their lab rats. It's cruel. How did they source these kids?"

The thought flashed through Sasha's mind.

"From the protesting kids, of course. If they're criminals then they don't have to ask for their parents' consent," Zircon walked away toward the kitchen island and away from the table where the boxes of documents sat.

"So instead of sending Zora and Muse back to their parents they endanger their lives and send them to Turpeek," Zircon was talking mostly to herself, trying to get the details in her own head straight.

"They were free to go once the study concluded," Sasha walked closer to Zircon then, and continued, "they were in the territory to be reunited with their family. It wasn't a permanent thing."

"Sasha, they could've died. Most of these kids died," Amethyst spoke softly.

"I'm sorry Zircon, but you wouldn't understand the relief of not having to be in pain and willing to do anything to have it cured," there were tears in Sasha's eyes now.

"Look, I'm not calling you a bad person for taking treatment for the pain. I'm not saying that. But Cerplex is incredibly dangerous, potentially addictive and has an effect on the mind that we haven't even begun to fully understand. It's not called the suggestion drug for no reason. A person on Cerplex is at the mercy of whoever is prescribing it. In high enough doses scientists were able to convince a person to commit a murder," Zircon spoke very carefully, her tone gentle.

"What are you talking about?" Sasha sounded disgusted when he was talking to her but it was obvious from his thoughts that it was the idea of what she said and not her as a person.

"In the 2040s when the drug was being tested at the Maykis Industries science lab they were able to convince a human being to kill a room full of animals. He did so with his own bare hands. Unfortunately somewhere a video of this exist if you don't believe me"

Sasha was shaking now. Unable to stay on his feet he took a seat at the table.

"Your dad is a very dangerous man. What they're doing in the Bluebird Territory arm of TerraTech is very dangerous" Zircon held back no punches when she spoke.

"What do you want me to do?" Sasha rubbed his face, shaking and red in the face.

"I don't expect you to do much of anything. What's done is done. We cannot let anyone in our world who isn't meant for it. But I want you to understand where I'm coming from. You can't defend your father like this. Cerplex isn't candy."

"I know that. Don't you think I know that?" Sasha spoke in a carefully measured pace, he was trying to reign in her anger.

Sasha thought back to his days in his apartment. He was strung out on it, dazed and confused about how much time had passed and where he was. Just as he was about to think something else, he shut them both out.

"What are you trying to hide, Sasha?" Amethyst put the file down and pulled out a chair and sat down.

"I wasn't doing anything purposefully. I did care about the cause. I was just a witness."

"What the hell are you talking about?" Zircon couldn't stand his beating around the bush.

"A witness to what?" Amethyst pressed.

"The protest," Sasha said.

"You're gonna have to explain what you mean because you don't make any sense," Amethyst pushed the boxes to the side to get a better look at Sasha.

"My dad had me collect names of people protesting so they could send them back. I've seen the studies in his files. I just didn't know how they ended."

"You monster," Amethyst stammered.

"I was on Cerplex the whole time," Sasha's voice was feather light.

"You knew they didn't want to be sent back. You knew they wanted to stay with their families. You protested beside them. You had them thinking they were safe. That they could trust you. What is wrong with you?" Amethyst couldn't stop herself.

In one rough motion she pushed all the boxes to the side, knocking two on the floor.

"How? How could you??" it was a headache-inducing scream now. Amethyst couldn't help herself. She wasn't thinking. Her thoughts were just bright white lights. She was blind with rage. Zircon hadn't said anything in a few moments now.

"Zora? Muse? Are they anything to you? Was Zora just some fling to you? Did you ever really care about her?"

"I cared about Zora. We weren't in love but it was something."

"And Muse, you just used her feelings for you against her?"

"I didn't know. I didn't know she had those feelings for me. I know it's no excuse."

"You're going to tell them what you did and you are going to deal with the fallout," Zircon's tone was final.

Sasha was breathing heavily. It looked like a panic attack but Amethyst was in her own mind space that she really didn't notice until he was clutching at his chest.

The Truth

Amethyst

What would she say to them when they came? How could she even lure them into the house to hear something so horrible? Sasha was pacing back and forth in the living room and Muse had already texted that they were a few blocks away as they had stopped for coffee. Amethyst felt bad for them and really nothing for Sasha but disgust and shock. The day was nearly spent, the sun was halfway up in the sky and golden light painted every floorboard. When the doorbell rang Amethyst braced herself but it was simply the mail. A Manila folder for Zircon from Timothy and a bouquet of red roses had arrived and she sat both on the table. The boxes from yesterday were cleaned up and Amethyst took out the pertinent ones regarding Muse and Zora and sat them on the coffee table.

You have nothing to feel nervous about. You didn't do anything wrong.

Amethyst could hear the thought just out of earshot. Zircon was in the kitchen cleaning and Amethyst thought to clear her mind rather than to actually keep things sanitary. The pair arrived a few minutes later. They buzzed the bell and waited at the door, Sasha opened it and had them both sit down. Zircon emerged from the kitchen then, her hands looked raw from being underwater for so long.

Muse had her hair in a ponytail, and Zora was wearing a dark green dress, showing off her glowing dark skin. Upon Amethyst noticing Zora said she found it at a boutique near the hotel. Amethyst nodded and took a seat on the armchair on the right in front of the couch. Sasha looked at the pair then, he said nothing and Zora looked up at him, looking closely at his face.

"I have something I need to tell you both." He cleared his throat and took a seat, probably wanting to face them directly,"I haven't been honest with either of you at all."

Zora was shaking now, her body and more purposefully her head.

"I didn't go to the protest just to protest. I was there as a witness for my father."

"I knew it!" Zora shouted.

"I was on Cerplex the whole time. It's not an excuse but it's the truth."

Muse's thoughts were dizzying. She was going through every single interaction they had had together and trying to piece together just when the lying had started.

"So you never cared?" Muse said flatly.

"I cared. People who went back got better, there was no denying that," Sasha sounded defensive.

"You didn't care about what we were fighting for. You only cared about what your father was telling you," Muse's voice portrayed no emotion.

"I thought he was helping people. I know now he was just prolonging everything."

"Explain what you mean, Sasha," Zircon was holding the bouquet of flowers and heading to the kitchen.

"He was trying to see if Cerplex could help those who had the gene. That's what was happening at Turpeek. He used it on you both," Sasha finished.

"I know about the Cerplex. I knew your dad had a hand in that too," Zora said, standing up. Muse grabbed her forearm then, urging her to sit down.

"He wasn't entirely in his right mind, Zora. He's caught up in this entire situation like we are," Muse's voice was soft.

"How could you buy this shit. He's a terrible person. He doesn't deserve our pity," Zora continued toward the door. Halfway there she turned.

"And you got Amethyst to sacrifice herself to save something so vile."

Zora left then. Amethyst could see her go into the SUV and sit in the back seat. She immediately went to her cell phone and began texting a number Amethyst didn't recognize. Amethyst stopped watching then and brought her attention back to the living room.

"You're the reason why we were arrested then. You could've done it sooner but you didn't though," Muse was mostly speaking to herself then.

The emotion in the living room had somewhat died down at that point. Amethytst left for Zora just to make sure she was alright. She couldn't drive in that emotional state. The tears were flowing when Amethyst came upon the SUV. Zora was hunched over. Amethyst sat in the back of the SUV with her and just sat there. Zora didn't immediately notice her presence. When she did she looked up, a half smile on her face. Zora brought Amethyst into an embrace. She was still shaking. Her body felt cold. Amethyst was worried she was getting sick. She felt guilty for ever being with Sasha. She felt guilty for ever inviting him to protest. She just felt an immense and heavy guilt. Amethyst instinctually shushed her and shook her own head.

"You did nothing wrong," Amethyst said. Zora only cried harder then.

Muse emerged from the house then and took a steady breath before walking towards the SUV. She sat in the driver's seat.

"Are you coming with us?" Muse said.

"Are you gonna be okay?" Amethyst asked Zora. Zora nodded yes. And sat up more, putting on her seatbelt.

"I'm here. We'll talk later," Muse said.

Amethyst opened the car door and left. Muse waved by as she pulled out of the driveway.

WARPATH

Zora

The thought didn't have to stay for long before she was set in her path. It was decided like one would pick out an outfit. She would kill him. She didn't say very much to Muse. She couldn't help how sad she felt and couldn't hide it either, but she could keep the anger at bay. The anger was unlike anything she ever felt. It was strange. She was so angry that she felt calm. Her body if she let the thoughts fester would vibrate with the anger but when she thought about her plan her body calmed. He had destroyed everything. He and his father had violated her body in ways she couldn't count. Their whole relationship was most likely fake and that thought cut her the most. He didn't deserve to have her body like that. He didn't deserve it.

The thing tripping her up was how would she do this. She had never even gotten into a fight with someone let alone kill anyone. She had thought about stabbing him until his body stilled. She thought about taking him to a lake and pushing his head until the bubbles stopped. Zora felt nearly gleeful about the prospect of him being gone. No one else seemed to understand her anger. Amethyst and Muse both seemed to have forgiven him or partially absolved him. Muse had gone to bed an hour ago and Zora was still up in the kitchenette staring at a kettle thinking about the ways she could get close enough to him to kill him. The anger would sometimes disrupt her vision and she had to temporarily go to another thought. She hated this. It felt like it took up precious time.

The kettled screamed and Zora got a mug from the hook below the cupboard. She decided to make chai. Her mouth felt dry. When she finished the tea, she took off her dress and joined Muse in the single king bed. They would try to get a double tomorrow, but this is all they had available for the past two days.

The sun was encased in a sheet of dark gray clouds filled with rain. It was a dreary day. When she got up she discovered Muse was already gone. Probably to get continental breakfast. Zora slid her green dress over her and slid on her mules. Taking her brush from her bag she made a few strokes to remove the look of "bed head". Down the restaurant area of the hotel was a buffet style breakfast set up. Muse was already seated and picking at a plate of eggs and home fries. She didn't notice Zora until she was standing right before her.

"Good morning, good to see you up and about," Muse said, taking a bite of her eggs.

"Get some food, sit with me," Muse said.

Zora got the same thing that Muse did, not wanting to think much about anything else and sat down. They ate in silence for twenty minutes before Muse said something else, interrupting Zora's murderous fantasies.

"I don't want you to misunderstand me. I don't forgive what he did. I just like the whole truth. Things aren't that black and white. He's still a horrible person," Muse said.

Zora didn't know what to say to that, so she nodded yes and continued eating, feeling ravenous. She barely ate yesterday.

"Are you listening to me?" Muse said.

"Yes, I heard you. I don't forgive him either. But I don't care about his excuses."

"Cerplex is—"

"An *excuse*," Zora's voice was firm. She didn't want to hear any more about how powerful of a drug it is or anything adjacent to that. She didn't care.

Muse didn't press her. She knew how broken up she was, and Zora guessed it was her way of being merciful.

Back in the room Muse turned on the news. Zircon was the first thing she saw. The newscasters were talking about the latest celebrity couple.

After much speculation, Zircon Millen and Timothy Talis have announced their engagement over social media.

"I didn't realize how big a deal this all was, every news channel is looping the same story," Muse said.

Zora nodded yes and sat on the bed.

"What's that on the crawler?" Zora said.

The bar flowing at the bottom of the screen had a list of names. Once it looped it came across again. In bold letters, LIST OF FALLEN ADULTS.

"Was there more?" Zora was distressed, she hoped it was old names and not new ones.

"No no, I recognized some of these names. It's gotta be the same people," Muse said.

"Where did you find the names?"

"A forum. It's invite only."

"Invite me?"

"Sure."

Zora spent the better part of the morning looking at the forum, each thread she went through she couldn't fully understand. They spoke in a coded language. It wasn't until the third or fourth page that she began to pick up on the meanings.

"Is this what you used when you would protest?" Zora said.

"Some of the time. Not everyone on it was involved in the cause. Some people just went back. They had to make rules against people judging them."

"Oh."

"Yeah."

"When I went on the forums the first time it wasn't coded, not until the protest became more common," Muse said.

"You have a thread here?" Zora was surprised. Most of the named threads were about famous people.

"You have one too, I can show it to you if you like." Muse said, smiling.

"No thank you. I wanna keep that stuff behind me."

"None of it is bad. People think you're really bad ass for what you did. You had TerraTech officials shitting bricks thinking you were gonna go through with it," Muse still had a blindingly white smile across her face.

"That was bad. We shouldn't have even attempted what we did," Zora said.

"They were still gathering up kids to test on. We weren't as bad as them," Muse sat on the bed.

Zora didn't know if she believed that but she nodded yes just to put an end to the line of conversation.

"We can go out for dinner. I could really use something simple like a burger and fries," Zora said. Muse nodded yes and smiled.

NO WORDS

Sasha

A *week, 2 days, twelve hours and thirty-four minutes later…*

Inky blackness seemed to cover every dot of light in his vision. Her thoughts were so fast he couldn't react fast enough. In his lap was his own blood, deep red and hot pooling, bathing every white thread of his white polo in red. He heard Amethyst scream something, but he couldn't make it out. He remembered the feeling of the hard cold floor on his behind. His hand was still where the knife was, his fingers lightly brushed the cold metal. His headache was unbearable. When he tried to call out he lost all consciousness. The last thing he saw was Amethyst's thoughts shouting at him, looking at his body by the kitchen sink, half bent over the knife. There was so much blood.

SWITCH

Amethyst

 *few moments later…*

The thoughts just stopped cold and like a switch had been clicked on I could hear every single thought everyone had at all moments, without stopping. I couldn't hold back the scream that fought its way up my throat. Zora had run to the back of the house near the patio door. She was pacing now. I could feel every emotion she felt. Her thoughts collided with my own. My emotions of shock were competing for attention with her thoughts of anxiety. I felt like I might faint. My veins felt hot. My whole body felt hot. Zircon was calling emergency services and praying that he would be alright. I didn't have it in me to communicate that there was nothing that could be done. He was gone. She took a kitchen towel from the stove and held it against Sasha's slumped form. I kept trying to hear his thoughts but there were none. I left the kitchen for Zora. She walked backwards into the door and began with a weak hand opening the patio door.

"I'm not. Something had happened. I can't hear anything," my speech was fractured and light. Zora looked at me confused and finally opened the door. She let the door close behind her. The sirens jolted me out of my thoughts. I ran to the front door to let them in. Zircon was still with Sasha. She felt a pulse, but it was light. They asked no questions as I opened the door and led them into the kitchen. In no time Sasha was on a stretcher being loaded into an ambulance. The thoughts didn't stop or die down and I couldn't turn them off. Zircon could hear everything I did, and she shook her head in disbelief.

The police were on their way, and I could hear their thoughts as they drove down the road. That road was a mile away. I couldn't believe how far I could hear. But if I could hear from that far away then why wasn't hearing the neighbors? I realized then I was filtering out the thoughts without realizing it. I let in the police, and they went to the patio. They didn't say much of anything. They sat down on the patio chairs and watched Zora. The taller officer was thinking about how unfortunate it was that she would probably be in jail in her prime years. That was unless her contract was bought out. I wasn't focused on the conversation, but I couldn't help but to notice how softly they spoke to her as they put the cuffs on her wrist. She was loaded into the police cruiser and she was gone. Zora was shaking the entire time and kept thinking about the scene in the kitchen. I tried my best to not let her thoughts into my mind but my ability to block it out was hard. I couldn't calm myself. In those moments of calm, I realized I was able to block out some of the noise.

Zircon was still in the kitchen just standing there. One by one police showed up until the entire living room was filled with them. The chief asked Zircon a bunch of questions which she answered. I couldn't for the life of me remember all but one: "If you can read minds, why weren't you able to stop her?". Zora's mind was laser focused on one thing and one thing only and that was to stay by Sasha. It was all she thought of. And like a flash in the pan, she thought about grabbing a knife completely out of context. Zircon, unable to still her own mind, used my thoughts to answer the officer.

I went to my room then, feeling sick to my stomach. When I laid on my bed all I thought about was how I was just talking to him, and he was just here. And now he was headed for the hospital alone. I was grateful that Muse wasn't here, and she would only hear it later, much later. It was such a horrific thing to watch happen and I didn't need any more thoughts in my head. I allowed myself to cry. The sound of my wails bouncing off the walls. Zircon was getting into her SUV and was about to leave but she texted me. I could see the text from her thoughts. My phone was still in the living room.

Give me a minute, I thought.

The sun was beating down on us as we wove around the backroads to the small countryside hospital. A police cruiser was parked in the lot. When we got inside there were more officers all around bed eight, talking to each other. They almost didn't let us see him until we explained to the doctor, we were distantly related. I instantly appreciated the gift of being able to read minds because I wouldn't have known otherwise that she was one of us. I was able to tell her that we were of the same family line based on our matching gifts. Dr. Kirk understood then and began explaining to use all that she did when he came. She spoke only in past tense. Her thoughts matched and didn't let on to what happened. Zircon sensing something was wrong began to get anxious.

"We tried everything we could, but it wasn't enough. He had lost too much blood."

I knew this. There was a big part of me that knew this. He was gone and I had developed some kind of super ability, my powers no longer splintered between two. Zircon, hearing my thoughts, couldn't hide her thoughts of relief. Sasha was no longer Half-blessed, and I was no longer a dead end. This was what had to be done. The half-blessed had to die. There was probably nothing his parents could've done, but now they were most likely stuck alive. Zircon and I went to his bedside, they had removed the knife. His hands were bandaged up. He looked like he was sleeping. His eyelids were lilac in color, he was incredibly pale. I could hear nothing, and I knew I wouldn't, but it still hurt me deeply. Zircon's mind was half blank as well. She was only thinking about being here, not expecting this was how her day was going to end up. The shock had dulled. She was just existing.

~

Zircon took the better part of the afternoon making arrangements for Sasha. I just listened to her make phone calls and watched her thoughts as she drove to the funeral parlor. I could've gone. I probably should've gone but I couldn't bring myself to do this. The next day would be the day we would call Marcus.

~

Zircon came back around 9 at night. She was holding a file and booklets from the funeral home. She expected me to help her make decisions. I have had no thoughts in my mind since this morning. I had completely let my mind run on autopilot. It was only keeping me breathing. I hadn't gone to the bathroom in hours. I didn't realize I had to go until I heard Zircon's thoughts intermingle with my own mind.

I met her at the door and helped with the papers she was holding under her arm.

Zircon thought we would still have to figure out who Sasha was at some point in time. It may not be in time for the funeral, but it would have to be a respectable amount of time after. In the back of her head, she thought about Zora. It wasn't in a judgmental way but horror in the act. She still couldn't believe that Zora would do that. There was another thought under that one, but Zircon didn't let it finish before she went to another thought about how she was hungry and hadn't eaten at all today.

~

I couldn't sleep that night. Too much of Zircon's thoughts got tangled up in my own. I texted Muse, telling her to come up when she could. She had gone back to Crow Feather when Zora told her to. I hadn't explained to her why she should come back. I would do that in the morning when my mind was clearer. I turned on the news and watched it until three in the morning. When I was about to turn it off the news had broken that a murder had occurred in Diamond Sea. Sasha wasn't named but Zora was. Her full name was in large bold letters. I half expected it to not hit the news, in the Crow territory though there didn't seem to be any laws that dictated against naming minors involved in crimes. In the Bluebird Territory there were countless, the cameras didn't even face them if the trial was televised. Anyone who leaked their photo to the press got a hefty fine and sometimes even jail time.

AFTERMATH

Amethyst

My phone felt slippery in my hand and also warm as if it had been overcharged. Muse's contact card was pulled up in my phone and I was debating with myself if I should call now or later. I hoped she wasn't watching the news, but Muse was the type of person to be deep within the news. She didn't merely watch it. She compared articles, read reports et cetera et cetera. When she wasn't reading the news, she was surveying the boards for more information. Not all of it was accurate but she looked for other things to corroborate what people were saying. I called…nothing…nothing…and then the call connected. No sound on the other side of the phone for a moment until I heard Muse yawn into the phone.

Yes!

Are you okay? I need you to come to Diamond Sea.

I saw. I know. I don't know if I'm comfortable coming there. It's just too much at once. There's nothing I can do there.

Her tone was utterly dismissive, and she sounded really irritated that I was calling. But what else would I do? She was Sasha's friend too. The least I could do was call and let her know when he was going to be buried.

I need you here, Muse. Can you come for me?
Let me think about it, okay?
Sure, no problem.

The call disconnected then, and I accepted then that she probably wasn't going to call back. She didn't want to be involved. Zircon was still thinking about the arrangements. She had called Sasha's adoptive dad; Marcus and he was too distraught to talk to Zircon much. It was a moment in which I wished I could read minds through the phone. Who knows what he could be thinking about. It was partly his fault. Sasha wasn't totally absolved either. It was greater than merely a mess. Marcus would arrive tomorrow morning and he would attend the funeral the day after. I decided to myself that I would try to say something at the funeral. My brain couldn't put words together. I was stuck on thoughts about how he died, and my brain still hadn't fully processed what transpired. I couldn't remember immediately was he was before any of the 'lost children' stuff happened. It was like the 'before times' were completely lost. I could remember bits and pieces. I remembered March 3rd like it was yesterday. It felt like that was when a new part of my life began.

Marcus brought with him a ream of paper having to do with Sasha. Since he had the mutated gene, he was technically a Crow though none of us knew who his parents were. Sasha belonged to the state and as a consequence he was assigned to a guardian even though he was gone. The guardian, Mr. Heart would have custody of his remains for four years but Marcus had made an under the table deal with Mr. Heart so Marcus could bring back his cremated remains back to the Bluebird Territory until they found his biological parents. I could hear how much he didn't want to make the deal, but Marcus was grateful to

have whatever time he was granted. It made no sense to me. He was
gone.

The programs for the funeral arrived shortly after Marcus arrived.
They were printed on ecru heavyweight paper. Zircon had paid for
part of the funeral. It was clear to me from her thoughts that she felt
guilty for making Sasha bare his guts to Zora and Muse. Zircon still
found it confusing. She had no idea how unstable Zora was as it wasn't
evident from her thoughts by a long shot. The picture they used was
one I took years ago, in front of the railing at the train station near the
Littlewood satellite campus. I had only gone there one time to take a
French exam. He was four years younger in the picture.

START

Muse

Merit had gone to the kitchen to clean and Muse, feeling lonely, went with her. Merit paid no mind to Muse and just continued clearing the table of breakfast from earlier in the day and cleaning the other marble countertops. When the cleaning was done, Muse told Merit that she could go out if she wanted. The truth of the matter was Muse didn't want to be alone, but she also didn't want to be perceived. The two needs clashed with each other. Merit nodded and left an hour later wearing her casual clothes.

Muse wandered around the house like a ghost. Drifting from room to room simply to look in them and touching the things she found. When she arrived at her parents' bedroom, she resisted the urge to look through anything. In her bones it still felt like they were still alive and sick though her common sense knew otherwise. It didn't feel like more than a month had passed since she entered the territory. It felt like only a few days had lapsed. Muse twirled her long curly black hair around her wrist, feeling the straggler hairs get stretched out and pop out of the follicle brought her back down to Earth.

A day ago, she got a copy of Merit's prisoner's contract. It stated she had a year left in her contract until she'd be released from servitude. It also listed how much Merit was 'worth'. Nearly six million a year for the past seven years. Merit was only 27 years old, what could she have possibly done at 20 to get her a seven-year sentence? The thought haunted Muse's thoughts for the better part of the afternoon.

The call from earlier in the morning was still circulating around her mind. She knew she should start driving to Diamond Sea, but Muse really didn't want to face the reality that Sasha was dead. A funeral made it too real. She didn't feel very much at the moment, and she didn't want to get written off as a crazy person or a terrible friend for not caring enough. She also didn't want to see Marcus. While he hated him before, now she was truly terrified of him. Turpeek was the worst experience of her life. It felt like jail. Anyone capable of doing what Marcus was doing was a sadistic asshole. Muse didn't know if she would be able to control herself if she was in his presence. It wasn't uncommon for her to do things without thinking about the consequences. She was better than when she was in high school but it was still bad.

Muse didn't bother to fold her clothes. Half of them still had the tags on. She borrowed a weekender back she found in the closet on the third floor. It must have belonged to one of her parents. She wasn't thinking much of anything when she drove. It was nearly 1am.

She turned on the radio and listened to the newscaster talk about the stabbing that occurred just days earlier. Zora's name wasn't mentioned much after that early morning breaking news but the language they were using was the kind that absolved her somewhat of the guilt. They called it an apparent crime of passion. Muse didn't know what they would do with her in this territory but if she were in the Bluebird Territory, she would not see the light of day again. In the Crow territory it seemed to be either jail time or servitude which in reality meant slavery by the high-ranking families that could afford it. Muse didn't know how to think about what Zora did. She understood the anger but not the act. Muse cared about Sasha as a friend. The feelings were constantly conflicting with each other. Though in her heart she felt guilty whenever she would think of Sasha.

It was 3:45 am when she pulled into a drive thru to order some food. She hadn't eaten since 5pm that night when Merit cooked. The drive thru had a code to scan to one's phone that showed the menu and allowed one to order from there. Muse was grateful she didn't have to talk to anyone. Once she ordered, it gave her the estimated time of fifteen minutes for her food to be done. A voice from the cylindrical speakers told her to drive forward.When she drove up to the window, she noticed the lights in the back of her were turning off.

The girl in the window had vibrant blue hair and equally blue eyes. Muse couldn't help but to gawk. She had never seen that shade before, and it didn't look like contacts. Her eyes didn't have a glossy look to them.

The girl nodded and turned back to the screen below her. Muse drove further into the lot and into a parking space. Muse felt incredibly awkward. She rarely ever drove and now she was driving late at night in a strange territory alone and eating strange food. They were burgers but they smelled strongly of a spice not typically used in her territory that she could not name. It tasted better than it smelled but left her tongue with a numb sensation from the spice.

The sun was starting to rise when Muse was approaching Diamond Sea, the orange light intermingling with the gray tint over the water. When she pulled into the driveway, she was relieved to still see the cars there. When she disembarked, she saw a light on the top floor turn on. She could've sworn she heard Amethyst say something, but she wasn't sure. The sound of footsteps was unmistakable. The front door swung open, and Amethyst ran to Muse, arms wide open and gathered her up in a tight embrace. Amethyst said over and over again *I'm sorry.* Muse couldn't respond. She didn't understand why Amethyst was apologizing. She didn't hurt Sasha. If anything, Muse thought it was her who should've kept a better watch out for Zora after Sasha had admitted what he did. Zora was already so angry before anything had happened and Sasha had given her reason.

"I should've stopped Zora, I'm sorry Amie."

Amethyst didn't respond to what she said. She stopped the hug and then shook her head, her features a little subdued.

"You wouldn't have known. There's something I want you to know."

"Know what?" Muse didn't want any more bad news.

"I can read minds and when Zora came, I couldn't even hear what her intentions were. She acted normal until she hurt Sasha."

"Can you hear what I'm thinking about right now?"

"Everything. All the time now. Well, if I could focus, I could filter it out."

Back in the house Muse was surprised the familiar location made her feel more relaxed. She didn't know it all that well, but she knew where a few rooms were and that was enough. She realized then that she still had to get changed into something more formal. She grabbed the bag from the car and went to the bathroom. Amethyst went to another part of the house. The black dress was something she found in her mother's closet. It still had the tags on it. She almost didn't want to wear it when she saw the price. It was $23,093Z. Muse decided to wear it because it was what would be expected from her. There would probably be news there and she didn't want her reputation to forever be the girl who nearly destroyed Hunter's Point Mall. She didn't want to be a Janis either, but she had no choice in that. The dress was a near form fitting wool poly-blend with a white collar. She put on pearls she had also found and black heels. This wasn't the first time she had worn heels. She often wore heels in high school but that was years ago. Muse didn't bother to look at herself in the mirror. But instead pack the rest of the things inside her bag and headed downstairs. Amethyst was wearing a skirt with knife pleats and a thin black sweater with a white blouse underneath, it's white color poking out. Zircon wore a long sleeve black dress with black heels. They took Zircon's car to the funeral home.

The parking lot was filled with cars. Muse recognized Dean Davis's small yellow car. All the other cars she didn't recognize. People came out in droves and there was a bit of a traffic jam at the front doors. If any of these people knew what Sasha had done, she wondered if they would still come but Muse remembering what Amethyst had said tried to keep those thoughts at bay.

The funeral home smelled old. The floors were carpeted in burgundy with matching drapes. The same shade of Maykis burgundy. The matching chairs were organized in rows with a big aisle between them. Muse was grateful she couldn't see a casket but after she saw there wasn't one, she was confused.

"He was cremated," Amethyst answered.

"Before the funeral?" Muse whispered.

"Yes, it's what Marcus wanted."

"How does he get to decide?" Muse's voice raised an octave.

"There's no one else to make that call. Mr. Heart let him."

"Who's he?"

"Sasha's guardian."

"But he's not— "

"Doesn't matter," Amethyst interrupted.

A group of people started muttering and turning to their trio. Clearly, they were listing to the conversation. Muse found it irritating.

ONYX

Amethyst

Zircon pushed me toward a group of people she knew. They were old members of The Night Crows. They wore onyx rings. I didn't know much about what they did but Zircon made it obvious to me that they were to be respected. They both were old and weathered. The man had dark blue eyes and had to be over six feet tall, the woman on the other hand was tiny. She had a doll-like face and small delicate hands. Her white hair was long and fell to her waist.

"Amethyst," the woman said.

"Hello," I said, as I nodded.

"I'm Lorelei," she said.

"I'm Gavin," he said.

"Nice to meet you both," I said.

"We must catch up when we go to the house," Zircon said.

"We're so glad you were able to come home. It feels like it's been a lifetime."

It's been my lifetime. I smiled and nodded yes, unsure of what else to say. There would be a lot more of this. I would meet people all day and I found that very prospect draining. Zircon and Lorelei and Gavin started speaking in Crow and I took that as my cue to leave. Muse was standing by herself for a moment until Ms. Davis floated over to her. It was the standard niceties. Muse seemed comfortable enough, so I left her to walk to the other side of the room in the opposite direction of Marcus. I didn't want to see his face. I still could remember with crystal clear clarity him ordering Sasha to help him hold me down. I wondered if he remembered it. Marcus nonetheless could still see me clear across the room. In my mind's eye I could see him staring at me. He was also debating if he should say anything to me and if anyone would notice if he didn't say anything to me. He decided to say something despite all my wishing and he walked across the room. I was about to introduce myself to a group of people when he tapped his finger on my shoulder. I turned around and tried to smile the best I could. It was uncanny how much he looked like Sasha despite them not being related. The same emerald, green eyes, the same shade of blonde hair. It was like they were meant for each other. The only major difference was the cruel glint in his eyes was obvious whereas in Sasha's it was well hidden.

"How are you, Amie?" He said, his eyes tracing over my features.

"I'm fine," I said. I was resisting the urge to cry. I didn't want to seem vulnerable to him at all.

"It's okay to not be okay. This is hard," he said as he walked away.

And that was it. That was the whole interaction. It felt odd. I was ready to dig my nails into him and he left, just like that. I searched his mind for something more but there wasn't much of anything but anguish, pain…something deep and foreboding that I couldn't put a name too. He had wanted my DNA, probably to help Sasha and now that Sasha wasn't here anymore, what was there for him to do? My thought wanted to go further to include that Sasha was his reason for living but the thought made me feel guilty.

We were ushered to our seats and the service began. The lights were dimmed and a projected video showed up on the wall. It was Sasha as a toddler. The first picture was him sitting in a kitchen with only a shirt and underwear, jelly smeared on his face. The next picture was him slightly older, a much younger Marcus holding him up above the water. The photo after that was us, sitting together on a park bench, our legs too short to touch the ground. We were wearing Littlewood Academy smocks. After that picture I closed my eyes and waited for the somber music to stop. When I opened my eyes, the lights were turned on. Marcus was standing at the front thanking everyone for coming. I didn't want to listen to any of this. I searched for Muse, but I didn't see her.

"I would like to thank you all for coming to the celebration of Sasha's life. I am, like many of you, sorrowful by how soon this is happening. Sasha was the kindest kid— "he trailed off, tears staining his speech. His shoulders slumped and he looked down. Taking a few shaky breaths he continued, "he was always trying to be a good friend. He was an obedient son and a good student though sometimes he didn't exactly do what he was supposed to. He had so much passion and cared for Amethyst like a sister. I...I don't know what else to say but I am grateful to have had him in my life." Marcus left the podium and took a seat next to Zircon. The room was quiet, but eyes were all over me. Everyone thought the same, when would I say anything. I got up and strode over to the podium. My mouth felt dry, and my legs felt like cooked pasta. I must have looked unsteady because Zircon held her arms out as if she would be able to catch me. I stood up straight and looked at the faces that I could see over and over again in every ones' thoughts. I cleared my throat and said the first thing that came to my mind.

"I loved Sasha...and none of this feels real. I tried my best to be a friend to everyone at once, but Sasha was always something more," as I spoke, I realized how romantic it was beginning to sound so I added, "he was like that brother I never had. If I needed someone I could talk to or just someone to keep me company, he was there and he wouldn't leave until I was okay." It was all true but blaring in my head now was Muse's thoughts. She had left the bathroom then and was watching me at the other end of the room. She was angry and she was fighting everything in her to say something about what Marcus and Sasha had done. I shook my head no and she looked down in shame. A few confused mutters floated to my ears, and I left for my seat.

Zircon went up only to ask if anyone else wanted to say anything and Ms. Davis did but didn't and she gestured to the back of the room where the waitstaff were putting out refreshments. I walked up to Muse and grabbed her by the hand. Taking her over to the lobby area of the funeral home. She knew what this was about without me even saying anything.

"Don't even think about it, not now. I know trust me, Muse. I know. But if you say anything, they're gonna look at you like you're a crazy person," I whispered to her.

"I was just thinking about it. I wasn't going to do it. I can control myself. But I know you've been thinking about saying something. I saw the way you were looking at Marcus. You looked like you could kill him," Muse whispered back, hard.

"I do. Don't think I don't. But if were gonna do anything of note we have to play by their rules. We can't just interrupt a funeral service."

"What do you suppose we do?"

"I don't know but not what you were thinking. Look, we both come from money. There has to be something we could do."

Zircon was looking at me now. Zircon thought, *don't do anything without consulting me.* I thought back, *I won't.*

"What?" Muse said.

"Zircon just basically told me to behave," I said.

"Wait, she's clear across the room, how did she? Can she?"

"Yes, she can."

Back at the house, a picture of Sasha was on display. Not everyone came over for dinner but a fair amount of people. Ms. Davis had gone to her hotel; she had a plane ride early in the morning. Muse was still thinking about announcing to everyone what they had done, and it was exhausting. Zircon was in the kitchen taking a breather. I sat at the top of the stairs with Muse and listened to the conversations that drifted through the air. The day had taken so much out of me that I was running on fumes. I looked over to Muse, watching her facial features twisted up in anger. I understood why she was so angry. Marcus and Sasha treated our kind like some science experiment and the experiment had gone horribly wrong. It was like a bomb had decimated in the middle of our lives and nothing would make it right. I thought then about what the officer had said about if Zora's contract was bought out and a new fear had seized my thoughts. What if Sasha's parents, his real parents had bought out Zora's contract? What then? I didn't know how any of it worked. And I wasn't ready to ask Muse to do some digging to find out how the process would work. I guessed that Zircon might know but apparently it was a Janis family tradition to buy out prisoners' contracts.

Zircon thought, *I wasn't thinking about that but now I worry. We'll talk about it when everyone leaves.*

The house was empty with the exception of us. We spent the better part of the night cleaning up all of the paper cups and small paper plates that were left behind. Muse noticed a change in my disposition and asked me what was wrong. I didn't answer her until we were out on the patio.

"I'm afraid for Zora," I admitted.

"Well, yeah, she's probably going to prison," Muse said.

"Well, what if she doesn't and someone related to Sasha buys out her contract?"

Muse shook her head, "wait a minute, you don't think someone would do something so cruel?"

"I do, Muse. I do."

Muse thought about how Merit had a seven-year sentence at only twenty and she wondered what she could have possibly had done.

"I don't know but what ever her crime was had to be bad to get that long of a sentence," I said.

Muse nodded and took a seat. I did as well. Zircon's thoughts grew louder and louder until she was out on the patio along with us. She had printed off something and was holding her place in the pages with her pointer finger.

"Zora's listed as a prisoner up for servitude," Zircon said flatly, her voice lighter than usual.

"How could that happen so fast?" Muse said.

"Trials happen that fast," Zircon said.

"How many…years did she get?"

"Seven," Zircon said.

"How much would that be?" I asked.

"Ten million per year is the starting bid," Zircon said.

"There's a bid on her?"

"Yes," Zircon said, as a single tear slid down her ruddy cheek.

Muse asked if she could see the paper and she turned to the page were all the Z's were. Zora June Jo'nest was listed, along with the name Zora June Peartree in parentheses. Next to it was a phone number.

"What's the phone number for?"

"To get a ticket for the party where you can make a bid," Zircon's voice broke on the word *bid*.

Muse thought about what a party like that would be like. Would she actually see Zora there. Muse stalled her thoughts and then thought about being on the patio, trying to push the images out of her mind.

"You would see Zora there and anyone else who has a similar starting bid. Her bid is huge though. I wouldn't be surprised if the Maykis family was there. We can only bid one, maybe two million above the starting bid. Muse, do you know what your resources are?"

Muse shook her head. She didn't know. She only knew how much Merit had cost. The entire conversation was making her nauseous.

"If you want to save Zora from that fate then this has to be a group effort. We'll put in 12-13 million per year in if you can match it. I can't imagine anyone outbidding us."

Muse nodded, unsure if what she had.

Zircon took out her cell phone and began dialing the number. The automated voice came on and said: *This is for tickets to bid on Zora June Jo'nest, Zora June Peartree. If this is correct press, 1, if not hang up and dial the number of the prisoner you would like to bid on.*

The starting bid is 10 million Z per year for a total of seven years. Press 1 if you understand. 1, How many guest, please use the keypad, 4, Thank you. Good bye.

Just then the tickets appeared as a text, each text with its own QR code.

Muse was shaking now, and Zircon tried to comfort her. She wouldn't allow it. She moved her hand from her shoulder. In her mind she was fighting with the words and the images of biding on her best friend. Of watching others bid on her best friend. But Muse thought if she didn't do it that she would regret it for the rest of her life. She couldn't lose another friend, Muse thought.

I didn't realize how tense my body was until I tried standing up to go to the bathroom. I left them there on the patio, the thoughts still following me. I saw in Zircon's mind's eye that the party would be this Saturday at the Talis Manor. Zircon didn't tell Muse this. She was going to tell her at a later time.

Muse would stay with us until the party. Zircon remade the bed in the guest room for Muse. There wasn't very much time between when she closed her eyes and when she entered a dream-state. I was grateful to not have to watch her all the time and just see the pretty pictures that were floating around in her head. I was glad her dreams were peaceful, she deserved as much.

THE NIGHT

Amethyst

Zircon spent the better part of the afternoon getting us ready for the night. She had straightened my hair and fixed it up into an ornate bun with two small diamond hairpins on either side of my head, keeping the stray hairs in place. She curled Muse's hair for her. And for both of us she outfitted us in some of the most lavish dresses in her closet. I wore a deep emerald- green dress and Muse was wearing a vibrant orange dress with spaghetti straps. Her breast were very obvious in the dress. Muse had sorted out with her banker about her financial capabilities, and he basically stated she could more than afford to make the bid of \$84-\$91 Million Z on her own if she wanted to, but it would be fiscally sound if she did it together as well. The banker sounded surprised that she was bidding that much on a prisoner, but he didn't further question her. I guessed realizing it wasn't his place. Muse looked so grown up. I mean she was a grown up but there was a regal air to how she carried herself. As Muse was putting on her light silk shawl that matched her dress, Zircon took the chance to tell Muse where we were going.

"It's not too far. It's at the Talis family manor in City Center."

This City Center was the main city Center, not the one just outside of Diamond Sea but further down.

"Your fiancé?" Muse said.

"His childhood home at least." Zircon continued.

"Makes sense. He's powerful, you're powerful. I see." Muse said, almost muttering to herself.

"Are you okay?" Zircon asked.

Muse nodded yes and swept a curl behind her ears.

***

City Center was a few hours away by car. On the ride up the air changed from its' grey tint to a deep blue. The air also smelled less fresh, the smog appearing right in front of us. The same quadrant design was apparent from high up the hill were we were as we drove down. I was able to tune out most of Muse's thoughts, giving her some privacy but I checked in periodically, mostly out of fear that she would do something at the party. The city looked magnificent. The tall sailboat sail design of the steel and glass building made it look as though it was wading on a sea of illuminated glass as the sun was setting. There was apart of me that was insanely curious about what this lavish party would be like. A mixture of anticipation and dread filled me. The only slave auction I had ever learned about happened hundreds of years ago and was in a history textbook. But this was different. Would there be people calling out numbers? Would we use our cell phones. I didn't want to picture it.

"Now when you get to the manor, I want you to stay close to Timothy and I," Zircon said as she took a left turn off the highway towards the local streets. As we went lower and lower to the local streets the glimmering city was out of sight and old gigantic mansions came into view with wrought-iron gates and large stone walls. Brown street signs indicated it was the historical district, something borrowed from the United States. The Talis manor was the grandest in the entire territory, taking up three entire blocks. It looked more like a castle than a manor, but I wasn't going to argue about semantics. It was made out of gray stone with a red brick and wrought-iron gate. The gate was open and we were in a line of cars going to the same place. There was at least five cars in front of us. When it was our turn the security officer scanned each of our QR codes and waved us forward. We were directed to a lot that was around the back of the building. We parked in the overfilled lot. Timothy texted Zircon that he could see her car and we met up with him. He wore a gray suit and a stone-colored tie which matched with Zircon's dress. My stomach began to sink in my gut when I saw how many people were walking into the mansion.

"They're not all going after Zora. There are nearly two dozen pris-oners' contracts up for bid," Zircon said.

I nodded and walked closer to Zircon and Timothy. Muse trailed behind as we walked up the steep stairs up to the manor, the small pebbles crunching under our heels. Inside there was soft music playing from speakers in ever corner. We were inside of a living room area. There were small groupings of chairs and sofas. At the other end of the room were refreshments and clipboards and small booklets.

"Muse?" Zircon said.

Muse hadn't thought anything out of the ordinary, so I was caught off guard by Zircon calling her name.

"Yes," Muse replied sheepishly.

"Timothy has agreed to join in our bid," Zircon said.

Muse didn't look phased and simply nodded her head yes and walked towards the clipboards wanting to get this whole thing over and done with as soon as possible. They were organized by name. Muse grabbed Zora's clipboard and booklet and walked back over to us. Timothy had bought two tickets, intending to bid on another prisoner as well. Zircon was hoping in her mind it wasn't a female and she was relieved when he grabbed the clipboard for a Freddy Mayweather. It was a short contract. Only two years. The name sounded so familiar to me.

A balding man appeared at the other side of the room near large white doors. Everyone gathered around him. Apparently knowing this song and dance.

. . .

"The room behind me contains the prisoners to bid on. If you've only secured a ticket to one or more you may inspect before making your bid. One by one please. Bids are done electronically using the number on the clipboard to text your starting bid. If you are out bid, you will receive a text to put in another bid. If not, you will get the contract in the mail and required to pay within 10 days," the man explained. The doors were open by two staff in black suits. We were ushered into a large ballroom.

***

Around the perimeter and in the center were large square marble pedestals. Every prisoner sat on their hunches. Their ankles and wrist were chained to every corner. They were like us, lavishly dressed but they weren't wearing shoes. There were just as many women as there were men. Zora was put in the very center of the room. Her hair had been braided into two long French braids. She wore a skintight silk Maykis Burgundy dress with a long slit down the side. It looked to be made for her.

"That's not good, look at her location," Timothy said.

"What do you mean?" I said.

"She's the most expensive prisoner here." Zircon said, her voice grave.

Zora noticed us then, her look was one of utter confusion. She was especially focused on Muse.

Muse was looking closely at her booklet now. Her bid was in bold letters. She was listed as Luxe. Muse thought about how sick everything was making her.

"So, I'll bid more," Muse resolved. The words fell on Zora's ears and she looked down, not wanting to see all the attention we were now giving her. I wished then I could speak to her but below where she sat was a sign that said no conversations with the prisoners.

There was a group of three people looking at Zora now, muttering under their breath about how she had killed a lost child. One of them said disgusting and went over to the man who was in the far right corner. Great. Perhaps no one wanted her because of the nature of her crimes. I had so many questions but I would wait until Zora was out of earshot. I could somewhat see the booklet in Muse's mind's eye. The first page was stats like hight, weight, age, and body measurements. The second page was her linage. She was distantly related to the Maykis family. The page after that was a list of people sponsoring the event, it was both the Maykis and Talis Family and Terra Tech. The final page was a list of rules:

1. No Speaking to the Prisoner during bidding

2. Purchases must wear Laura Bracelets for tracking purposes

3.Homes Must be outfitted with the latest Terra Tech or Maykis Industries security systems within 10 days of purchasing

Further guidelines can be found at PCAS.net. Muse used her cell to go to the link and discovered there was a long, very long list of rules about security requirements. But there wasn't much that concerned what you couldn't do with whoever you 'purchased'. What was glaring was the fact that prisoners agreed to this knowing that any chance of parole or a retrial was forfeited. Zora had agreed to this instead of prison. That was printed in bold letters before one even began scrolling to the bottom of the guidelines. I guess they had wanted to make people feel better about buying other people.

In the middle of my thought I saw a man float over next to us. He was looking very closely at our group.

"She's beautiful," He said. He wore a name tag that said Andrew Talis. His eyes were the deepest shade of blue I had ever seen. I realized then that everyone else had on name tags and I felt utterly out of place without on.

"I'll get them," Zircon said.

Timothy walked up to the man and they began to chat. They were cousins he answered to me in his head. Andrew commented that he was interested in a companion. Timothy nodded but in his head he was worried now. People who bid with the intention of looking for a companion often put in more than what was expected to secure their bid. Timothy didn't ask what his bid was and inside of my mind I was screaming.

Zircon had left and came back and Andrew still had not left, he still closely looked at Zora, taking in her whole body. He put in a bid on his phone for 12 million a year and walked away then.

Zora was looking up now, whereas when Andrew was there she was looking a way, not wanting his eyes on her own.

I then put in our original highest bid for thirteen million. Then there was an immediate ping that we were outbid. It was Andrew again. Timothy told me to put in a bid six million higher. I put it in and we were outbid. The man next to the refreshment table in the other room had put in a bid eight million higher. I looked over towards Zircon and she nodded, and she thought, put in a bid two million higher. So I did and we were almost immediately outbid by Andrew. Zircon internally said, fuck.

Muse was looking over her banking app, and after a a quick look she took out her own phone and put in a bid nine million higher and for a while no one outbid us. Andrew was debating with himself. He wanted to look over three other prisoners. But with a few quick keystrokes he bid fifteen million a year. Before Muse could put in another bid, a text stating the biding was over and listed the names for prisoners still without bids who would be taken to the auction hall in thirty minuets. My heart sank. Zora was really gone now and there was nothing that could be done. Andrew was walking back into the bidding hall again, leering at Zora on her pedestal. He was thinking about how much he couldn't wait to take her to bed and I couldn't hold it down then, the bile rose in my throat and I picked up my dress and ran toward the bathroom. I was grateful there wasn't a line. I was thankful I hadn't ate or drank anything recently or else I wasn't sure I would be able to make it. Muse was walking towards the bathroom and she went into the stall beside me. She thought really loudly towards me, *I don't think I can do this anymore. Be in the territory. I don't know what I should do because I have responsibility of Merit.*

Back in the bidding hall Timothy was feeling bad about not being able to buy Zora for Zircon.

"I—"I began, until a group of woman walked into the bathroom. I could see them fixing their makeup and adjusting their dresses.

"Did you see the girl who just ran in here. She got sick. Not in Kansas anymore, Dorthy," one of them whispered to the other. They laughed. I could see their name tags from their mind's eye. Lia Clover was the girl who just spoke and she was next to a Perci Weatherly who had vibrant blue hair that fell to her waist. Her eyes were the same shade as Andrew and it was clear to me that she must have been a Talis. Perhaps she was married.

Muse was grabbing at her dress, trying to contain her anger.

"Did you see the piece of eye candy on the back wall. 6'7, perfect Italian features. Did you have a ticket for him?" Lia said.

"No no, I'm looking for a girl maid. Someone to do my shopping and cleaning. Not that men can't but it's not really their nature. Plus I already have a boy toy. He has another five years on him," Perci said.

I was trying to keep my nausea at bay but it was so hard with the conversation happening. Lia had taken out a compact from her bag and was touching up her blush. She had light brown hair and light pink lips. Her eyes were a very light green. She was beautiful like everyone else here seemed to be beautiful. Nothing she was saying matched with the evil things she was saying. Muse got up then and realizing she had to go, used the bathroom. She left the stall after and quickly washed her hands before she left. The pair was still fixing their makeup. They talked about the dinner that would be happening later in the night.

THE DINNER

Amethyst

In the dinning hall was the stage where the auction would happen. I wanted to leave but Zircon advised against it. It had become the first event I had gone to since I entered the territory and as a result it was my introduction to society. Muse and I sat next to each other, Zircon and Timothy and his cousins Andrew, Jules and Leslie were on the opposite side of the table along with Andrew's wife Jin Hee. The band was playing smooth jazz and men with stun guns were arranging the five prisoners without bids onto chairs on the stage. The first one was a girl who could've not been much older than I was. She was tiny and her eyes were wide. The waitstaff was walking around from table to table taking the order of one of three entrees, chicken, vegetarian pasta or fish.

I kept thinking about calm things, like waves on the beach or lullabies to fend off my nausea.

Muse wasn't thinking about much of anything but being in the room. She wondered what the fish she ordered would taste like and how annoyingly loud the music was blaring from the speakers. She had mentally checked out and I was on my own. Everything was calm for now.

The same man from earlier reappeared and told everyone to take their seats. He did so with hand motions.

"The auction will start in a few moments. This auction will be live via a text message. You may come up to the stage to look over each prisoner as they are presented on stage by the handlers," He said. The man nodded to himself. He walked further to the left of the stage.

"The first up for auction is Charlotte Poll. Sentenced for three years for theft. Starting bid 3 Million"

The sound of constant clicks and pings was irritating. I tuned out the thoughts then, the sounds of people's thoughts were reverberating like an echo. The man pulled out his phone then.

"Bidding is closed. The winner is Victor Lively."

The wide eyed girl was taken off the stage then and taken to a door on the opposite side of the stage. I read her mind. She was panicking about going to this room. Her thoughts were like slush. The floors swayed beneath her feet. She had been drugged. She worried about them drugging her again for the ride back to the prison.

Andrew was internally kicking himself for not bidding on her. He wasn't expecting her to go that cheap.

Our meals arrived after the first action, the waitstaff putting our plates out in front of us. No one immediately started to eat, instead they took out their phones for the next prisoner to bid on.

Jin Hee was debating with herself on the next auction and she decided to not do it and put her cell phone away.

"Anything peaking your interest, Millen?" Andrew said to me.

I nodded no and took a bite of food to buy me time.

"Many of them went so fast, I couldn't keep up," Jules said.

"These are just the clearance bin at this point," Jin Hee said.

Leslie had his phone at the ready to make a bid on the next prisoner.

"The next prisoner is Fernando Miles. Sentence to two years for aggravated assault. Starting bid 2 million."

Leslie's fingers flew across the on screen keyboard on his device.

He had won him and sat back satisfied.

***

In the car not much was said. I sat in the back of the car with Muse and she was thinking over and over again about how she had lost two friends in a week. She was trying her best not to cry but when Zircon reached the highway she balled. I was numb.

"The Saved" Bonus Content